BETWEEN THE SPREADSHEETS

NICKY FOX

Copyright © 2018 by NICKY FOX

All rights reserved.

No part of this book may be reproduced in any form or by any electronic or mechanical means, including information storage and retrieval systems, without written permission from the author, except for the use of brief quotations in a book review.

Edited by: Virginia Tesi Carey

Proofread by: Marla Selkow Esposito

Formatting by: Affordable Formatting

Cover Designer: Kassi Snider with KassiJean Formatting & Design

Cover Photo by: Lindee Robinson

Cover Models: Johnny Morrish & Daria Rottenberk

Dedication:
For my real co-worker, Cindy. Go for it Girl!

1

"Just because I like pink frilly things, doesn't mean I'm void of depth or feeling. You can shove that misogynist judgment up your ass," I whisper-yell and walk away from the most infuriating man I've ever met. Usually people like him don't bother me. When I say "like him," what I mean is those guys with the dark clothes who read Stephen King and think they know everything about the world. Who have such deep thoughts that my preppy, simple mind can't comprehend. It's like the only way to be smart and deep is to wear black, hang out in a coffee shop, and be depressed and act uninterested all the time. I take joy in the simple things. Does that make me simple? I like pretty things. Does that make me superficial? I'm also female. Does that make me emotional and needy? I'm not trying to write some bitter diatribe on the inequality of women. Normally I'm able to brush guys like him off, but this man drives me absolutely insane.

"You can take out whatever's up your ass today," Dylan calls out at my retreating backside. I'm forced to work with a shaggy hair, grunge, hipster beard, ass wit, who is condescending at every opportune moment. Not that what he wears or looks like has any effect on how I see him as a person, but it's exactly the problem he has with me. Yes, I wear polos and pencil skirts with high heels. I curl my hair and want to look neat and tidy. It's a style I'm comfortable in and I feel looks best on me. I also happen to find beards super attractive. If Dylan wasn't so much of a schmuck I might see myself liking him. He's attractive, like hot actually. Bright brown eyes pierce through the dark brown hair that hangs in his face. His lips, God. His lips seriously turn me on. I mean they are encased in a grungy hipster beard. Not that I would ever even consider kissing him or doing anything with him. Dylan is vile. Although, he's passionate in what he believes in. It just so happens what he believes about me is all wrong.

There's more than meets the eye in the pink clothes I wear. I'm a sensitive person and I care about other people. In my line of work, you do need to care about your coworker's well-being. I'm passionate about animals and I love movies and children. I bet Dylan despises children. *No, I will not be quick to judge like him.*

When he spills words of equality and prejudice and then in the same breath he projects his inaccurate assumptions of me because of the way I dress or decorate my office, then what does that say about him? He's the same thing he's trying to rally against. Dylan hasn't even tried to get to know me as a person. He has no idea who I am or where I come from. I mumble to myself, "Don't turn around, don't turn around," but the pull I have to fight with him always wins out. "Dylan, remind me who you are named after again?" I chuckle to myself as I leave him in the breakroom.

It might sound like a lame comeback, but it pushes his buttons. Every time I mention that little nugget his hands ball up into fists and his mouth goes into a thin line. It's awesome. See, he is forever fighting the fact that his parents named him after the most cliché, moody, poet/singer ever . . . Bob Dylan. To him, it's like being a hipster named Finn or River. Dylan doesn't like being a walking cliché. I like to dig it in whenever he's really pissing me off, like today. It started off as a normal conversation like it usually does. We talk about work and the weather and suddenly it's *Clash of the Titans*. Most people steer clear of us when we're both in the same room. Our coworkers don't like being pulled into the hate vortex.

Today was no exception, and like me, he knows what buttons to push. The morning went something like this: I entered the breakroom, I acknowledged his presence with a nod, avoid, avoid, avoid and then he sneers at me. His nose scrunched up with his lip as he had a look of disdain on his face. Being the grown-up I am, I ignored it and went about making my morning tea. Then, he opened his mouth. "God, you even make your tea snooty." He's always the instigator.

"What is that supposed to mean?" I reply, ceasing the dunking of my tea bag.

"Black tea? Really who drinks it without cream, sugar,

or honey?" I know he's just doing this to get a rise out of me. I make my tea the same way every day. He's seen me make it every day. It's not like this is a new occurrence.

"Yeah, I like it black like your soul." I smile over the rim of my cup, but my victory is short-lived when I notice he's taken that as a compliment by the smile he's giving me. Fucker. If I had balls I would so want to teabag him right now. I adjust my diamond stud earrings, it's a nervous habit of mine.

He moves in close, like he has a secret to tell me. I lower my cup from the front of my face. He looks so smug. "At least I have a soul, princess." That's when I snapped. I metaphorically teabagged him with my words, mentally gave him the finger and got the hell out of dodge, because I was so close to pouring my hot tea all over his hipster bearded ass. I know it's petty and childish, but it's our thing. I secretly think he gets off on it. He always finds a way to antagonize me.

I walk by Cindy's desk. Hers is closest to the breakroom so she is privy to our adolescent banter daily. She gives me a knowing smile. I smile back and give her a roll of the eyes. She knows what I have to deal with day in and out. We work at a corporate accounting firm. It's not exciting, but it's stable and I love my job. I'm in HR. Unfortunately, Dylan was already working here before I got this gig. Even though he is a pain in my ass, he's really good at his job and he seems to love it. The hipster comes off as gruff and hard edged, but I've seen him with other people. He can be charismatic when he wants to be, friendly even.

The first time I met him, I thought he was lost. He came into my office to ask a question about his time off. He took one look at me and it went downhill very quickly. You'd think in my position he would schmooze me a bit, try and get on my good side. But no, it's not his style. His broad shoulders filling my doorway, I thought he was a maintenance guy. He looked like a guy that worked with his hands, his very large hands. I call him a hipster, but he doesn't really have the physique that I picture when I think of a hipster. He's not lean. He's brawny and muscular under that tight white dress shirt he wears. Dylan doesn't look like the type of guy that would sip a beer. I could picture a pint in his hands, the froth from the beer clinging to his whiskers. He has tattoos too. I've seen them when he rolls up his dress shirts. So hot.

I'm getting off topic here, but he's a massive, intimidating guy. He's probably used to people bending to his will. Unfortunately for him, I'm not like that. I'm stubborn, organized, and efficient. I don't like bullshit, which is something we have in common. If he could sit in my office for more than five minutes and talk about something other than what I'm wearing or my intellect being lower than thou, then we might actually be able to get along. He had the audacity to come in my office and say that I put his time in incorrectly. He spoke slowly so I understood him, and I spoke like a Neanderthal so he would understand me. And so, our wonderful work relationship was born.

I collapse in my chair, wondering to myself how a guy like that works in an accounting firm. I do know that he's a whiz with numbers. I think he was a child prodigy. Dylan gets away with a lot here because of it. Honestly, I'm surprised he hasn't gone out and created his own firm. On the other hand, he doesn't like dealing with the finer details, which I specialize in.

I glance around my beautifully organized desk. My office doesn't have a window, and so I try and cheer it up a bit with color and beautiful things. When I say color, I mean mostly pink. I'm obsessed with the color. I know, I'm such a girl. It's a cheery color. The most beautiful flowers to me are pink. I love flowers and I have some fake flowers on my desk. If I had the money I would have fresh flowers every day.

I'm not a type A personality all the way through but everything has to have a nice cute little place. I look at my large collection of sharpened pencils; that's like a bouquet there in itself. My cute little notebooks, Post-its, and calendar. These things make me happy. They make me feel relaxed and I'm able to do my job efficiently when everything looks bright and I have easy access to it. I added floral pillows to the blah gray chairs that came with my office and have calming pictures hung. After I finally unloaded all my office supplies, Dylan came by and had to comment that it looked like Barney threw up Pepto-Bismol. All the women and some of the guys say it looks really nice, so I just ignore his jabs and keep doing what I do. He can pass judgment all he likes, I'm not changing.

I've worked here for two years now and I love it. The job I moved here for didn't pan out. It just wasn't a good fit and after a year, I left and joined this firm. The people are great, well most of them, and I can see myself working here for my entire career. I love doing this kind of work and helping people. I also get to plan some of the holiday parties. That's my favorite, decorating for the holidays. Cindy and I are close for coworkers. We don't hang out a lot, she's quite a bit older than I am, but we talk on the phone after work sometimes. We like discussing the daily fights I have with Dylan.

"Andy, there's an emergency meeting being called. All staff need to go to the boardroom immediately." Before I can ask Cindy what's going on, she's moving on to the next office to inform them of the meeting. Shaking my head, I grab a pad and pencil to take notes. I don't think I've ever been involved in a meeting where the company as a whole was there. This should be interesting. It must have been impromptu as normally they send an email a couple days before.

2

"We've gathered all of you in here to inform you that the company has been bought out effective immediately. We were trying to get our numbers up in the last quarter, to no avail. I'm sorry this is so sudden, and we can't offer you more than two weeks' pay. We understand the strain this puts on you and we tried to talk the new company into keeping some of the staff, but I think they're going to be cleaning house. They wanted our big-name clients and now that they have them well, we are of no use it seems. Myself and John will take any questions you have at this time."

My life is suddenly in a tailspin. I've just lost my job. My mouth is still hanging open when I catch Dylan's eye. He looks solemn, but not upset. He must have some savings built up. I have none. I just managed to get all my bills sorted out, after racking them up through college. That was three years ago. I'm near tears. What the hell am I going to do? The meeting continues with some coworkers riling up and others sad and quiet. It seems like we are in the meeting for hours, when it's only been one. We are finally dismissed to gather our things.

Cindy's crying and I try to console her as we make our way to our desks. She has two kids and is a single mother. I really hope she has some savings. She lives in the suburbs and her home is paid for; that's at least something she doesn't have to worry about. We'll keep in touch and she'll keep me updated on her circumstances.

I moved here after graduating from the University of Alabama. That's where I grew up. I wanted to go to Chicago and stand on my own two feet without the help of my father. Since my mom passed away when I was young, my dad focused most of his energy on work. I send him a postcard on holidays but we don't really have a relationship. I still miss my friends from college. Since moving here three years ago, I haven't really made any friends apart from Cindy. I live in a bustling city and yet, I'm alone.

I rent a small studio in Lake View, an easy commute by the L to, well now my previous job. It's small but the rent is affordable. I've decorated it and made it my own. I have to get another job quickly, otherwise I'll have to go crawling back to Alabama a failure. I won't let that happen. I'm determined to come out on top in this city.

Ever since I saw the movie *While You Were Sleeping*, I've wanted to make the trip to Chicago. Sandra Bullock's character is a single girl in the city. Her parents are absent in her life as well. She falls in love at first sight with a man she meets at her job. How romantic. Of course, she does end up falling for the brother. I'm such a romantic at heart.

Luckily, I was able to live home during college and not have to pay for a dorm. I had a job at the local pizzeria and saved enough money to make the trip out to Chicago. It was luck finding a job as a secretary before I left. I worked there for about a year before I found this position. I wanted to become a career woman and then fall in love with a mysterious stranger. It's still a nice thought, but I've become a bit more jaded since I first had that dream. Right now, I'd be happy with just being able to afford my small studio.

Slowly packing my things into boxes, I think about what my next step will be. I need to update my résumé, scour the want ads, look online, and possibly hire a headhunter. This sucks. A figure looms in my doorway and it's the last person I want to see right now. Dylan is leaning against the doorframe with his hands in his pockets. I brush my hair away from my face and continue packing.

"Before you say anything, Dylan, I'm really not in the mood for any of our witty banter right now. All I have to say to you is good luck and have a nice life." See, I can be civil with him.

"Witty banter? Andy, that's funny." Never mind.

"Fuck you, you hipster brawny man. I was actually trying to be nice to you for a moment. Now, all I have to say to you is get the hell out of my office. I hope your life sucks." I'll be honest. I'm not used to cutting people down. So yeah, my comebacks might be a little childish, but they get the point across. I normally don't cuss at work either, but he seems to bring out the sailor in me.

"I don't believe I've ever heard you say fuck. I like it. Now, I have a few things to say to you. I have a job—"

I cut him off, "Of course, you do." The bastard is coming here to rub it in my face. What a jerk!

"Let me finish, Andy. For Christ's sake. I have a job for you."

I pause and look away from my boxes for a minute. His light brown eyes are focused on me. *He has a job for me? What?*

"Don't patronize me, Dylan. I'm really not in the mood. I'm sure whatever perverted position you have available for me can be taken up with the B.B.B. Now, please stop wasting my time." I shove my ivory desk calendar in a box and it crinkles. Ugh, I'm ready to pull my hair out! I might cry.

"ANDY!" I'm jolted by his raised voice. He quickly looks around and shuts my door. Dylan bends over and sets his hands on my desk. We stare at each other, eye to eye. "I'm being serious here. I think it's time I opened my own firm and I want you to help me start it up. You know all the legalities and the filing crap. I need someone like that."

I drop to my chair as he towers over me. He's offering me a job? I rephrase that in my head. He wants to continue to work with me, for him? This is insane.

"I can see the wheels turning in your head. Before you say anything you regret, it comes with medical and maybe an occasional lunch." He smiles at me. At least, I think it's a smile. He could be constipated. I can tell he's nervous though. I give him the side-eye. There's got to be a catch.

"Are you freaking crazy?" I reply. This guy is seriously out of his gourd.

"Now, Andy. I'm offering you a legit job here. Do you really want to call your new boss crazy?"

"New boss? I could never work for you. We'd kill each other. K.I.L.L." I use a slashing motion across my neck to emphasize my point.

The bearded monster moves to sit down and notices my floral pillow. He picks up the pillow and chucks it across the room. It lands in one of my boxes. I sneer back at him.

"Boss, work for, under, whatever, it's just semantics. I'm one hundred percent serious here, Andy." I don't think I've ever heard him say my name this much. It kinda makes me hot . . . but in an angry way. "Look, you have my cell on file. I already have some things lined up. I just need someone to handle the office details. I'm not good with . . ." He motions around my office and rests on some file folders. "The pay will be very good, more than what you're making here."

I cross my arms in a huff. "How do you know what I make here?"

"I've been here a lot longer than you have, sweetheart."

"First, if this is for real and you're not just jerking my chain for one last hurrah, then there will have to be some guidelines." I'm fuming.

"Guidelines for me? Uh, no, honey. I might not call myself your boss, but I will be. I don't need to follow shit."

I ignore his comment and keep going. "First, you will not call me, sweetheart, honey, sugar, puddin' pop, or anything resembling food, fruit, candy, or dessert."

"Puddin' pop?" He laughs.

"Second, I'll need my own office away from you, to do my work properly." I wait for him to say something. When he doesn't, I move on. "Third . . . I don't know. I'll make this up as we go along. I'll be your equal as a human being. I will not tolerate you talking down to me. Understand?" I talk a big game, but on the inside I'm somewhat excited about this turn of events. "How many people will be at your firm?"

He points to himself and then me. "Just you and me. I'm starting off slowly. We'll see how it goes from there. Eventually, I see us branching out and hiring more people, which is where you come in."

Hell, I don't know if this will work. I have nothing to lose though. It's a job offer, I can't really say no. This jackass better not be wasting my time or I'll kick him in the balls.

"Okay." I hold out my hand to seal the deal. He takes my small hand in his and gives it a firm tug.

"Nice doing business with you, Miss Lauder." He has that smug grin on his face. I always want to slap it off. Before he leaves my office, I have one last question for him.

"Mr. Ryder, will I have that offer in writing?"

"If you write it up, sure." Dylan strolls out of my office without a care in the world. This morning I was cursing his name. Now, I'll be working exclusively for him. This is seriously an alternate universe I live in.

3

Looking up at the building of the address Dylan gave me, it looks like housing. I check the address I wrote down again and it's correct. He better not be doing all this as some ploy to get me in his apartment. Maybe I'm just meeting him here so he can take me to the new office? We could grab coffee on the way. I skipped my coffee this morning. I was so nervous about this whole scenario. There were butterflies in my stomach and I didn't think drinking coffee was a smart idea. I don't have a car here in Chicago so I mostly walk everywhere or take the L. Occasionally, I get an Uber, like today. With all my office supplies I wouldn't have been able to walk. Luckily, this address is not too far from my studio so I can walk here from now on and save myself the money. It's a much nicer area than Lake View.

Making my way through the lobby, I ask the doorman if I can leave my stuff with him. I hit the elevators and punch the button for the sixth floor. As I ride up I think about my conversation with Cindy last night. She thought it was great Dylan offered me a job. Then I asked her if she'd been present the last two years in our office. She's all for this new position. I know she doesn't say it, but she likes Dylan. Cindy thinks under that rough exterior he's actually a good guy. She's crazy. I think she just tries to see the good in people. She's really the good person. Cindy hasn't found a position yet, but she said she's okay and for me not to worry. See what I mean about good? Cindy's the best. I can't imagine how difficult this change will be for her. I just hope she can find something quick.

The doors open and I go to number 601. There are only three doors on this floor, so this space should be large. This is promising. I straighten my pencil skirt, adjust my bag, blow my bangs out of my face and knock lightly on the door. There's no answer. I knock more forcefully.

There's shuffling on the other side and the door unlocks. I'm stunned to see a woman half-dressed answer the door. I glance down at the address again. It's correct.

"Sorry, I must have the wrong address. I'm looking for Dylan Ryder."

She yawns and gathers the too big dress shirt wrapped around her. The woman's long dark brown hair is hanging over one shoulder. Her legs are bare and I'm sure she's just wearing panties under that shirt, at least I hope she is. She waves me in. I look around the door quizzically. A large hand grabs the top of the door and moves it open wider. Dylan's face comes into view, and that's when I notice he's not wearing anything. He's covered with a sheet around his waist and nothing else. I give him daggers and turn on my heel to walk away. I knew it. I fucking knew it. He played me.

"Hold up, Andy, just a sec."

I make it to the elevators and jam down on the button multiple times to release some anger. The nerve of him rubbing whatever that was in my face. I'm the stupidest woman alive to have fallen for his job offer. He's lucky he still has his balls right now. Desperation, that's what I'm blaming this on. I had a weak moment and he offered me an out and I took it. Now, I just need to organize and prioritize, make some lists. I'll be on the up and up in no time. The douche nozzle makes his way to me, almost tripping over his sheet a few times. "I slept in. I forgot to set my alarm last night. I know this makes a bad impression, but I have everything set up and waiting for you. I just need . . ."

"Some pants," I deadpan, not giving one iota what the hell he did last night. The elevator dings and the doors slide open. I move inside and he follows me. Wow, the jerk really doesn't want to keep his balls. Dylan's basically naked in the elevator with me. I look up at the floor numbers and try to keep my eyes from wandering. He looks really hot in a sheet. Even though he's a dick. I wonder what he'd look like in a towel?

"Andy, I know this looks bad, but I swear it's all professional. I just overslept." Yeah, right.

Crossing my arms over my chest, I give him an encouraging smile. He looks a little terrified by this, which he should. "Why are you sleeping at the office, Dylan?" I say in my sweetest voice. This should be a very easy question for him to answer. It better not be that he was breaking in his desk.

He squints his eyes, as if he's about to get slapped in the face. Which, I may oblige him. "It's my apartment." *Ding.* The elevator doors open. I huff and walk out toward the lobby. "But it's completely legit, Andy. I swear. You're annoying, but I wouldn't lie to you. I just need to get dressed and we can put this behind us."

I turn around to tell him off, when I see some type of fluid on his beard that looks like . . . "Oh, my God. Is that cum on your beard?" I gasp, pointing at it. Disgusting.

"What?" His tongue comes out and licks around the spot. "No, it's whipped cream."

"Ugh! Funny how you had to taste it first to make sure." What the hell was he doing with whipped cream? I don't even want to know.

He sighs. "I don't go down on one-night stands. Anyway, I'm sorry how this played out this morning. I'll get what's her name on her way, put some clothes on, and we can start over. What do you say?"

I turn to leave and escape this big fiasco. I mean, who does he think he is? This is no professional atmosphere. He was probably thrusting Miss Sunday Night in my face to show he can get a girl to spread her legs for him. Despicable!

"Please, Andy. Please. I really need you." Damn. He actually sounds sincere.

That *please* literally kills me. He's never uttered that word to me, even when he was trying to get two weeks off at Christmas last year. I can check out his "office" and see if everything is in order, and then make my decision. I turn around and face him. He looks ridiculous standing in the middle of the lobby with just a sheet hung around his waist. I'm sure passersby would think this is some lovers' spat.

I stare at his chest like a creeper. He's covered in tattoos. There are too many to concentrate on just one. Flanking his chest I see swallows in bright colors. There's a heart, a moth, a few skulls and stars, a wolf, a bear, coy fish, a lion, some arrows, and an owl just to name a few. Dylan is gorgeous. He's still breathing heavily from chasing me down here. My eyes travel down to where he clasps the sheet on his hip. I have to look at his crotch. I'm a woman and I'm curious. Since the sheet is white, I can see through it a little. There is definitely an outline of a large package down there. His hand comes into view and motions for me to look up with two fingers. I blush and jolt my gaze back up to his face. His hair is tousled, his eyes bright, and he has that smug grin on his face. Jerkface. He knows he looks good.

I march on over to him. He looks somewhat afraid of what I'll do. That makes me smile. He instinctively covers his dick. I cross my arms and give him another once-over. "This will not be happening again. If I am to work for you this needs to be a professional atmosphere. I don't want to work around some half-naked hipster who uses natural deodorant. You're on probation, Ryder." I walk to the elevator and he shuffles after me.

He chuckles. "Natural deodorant?" He raises his arm

in the elevator and sniffs his armpit. "I smell fantastic. I use Gillette."

I shake my head. "You smell like sex," I say with disgust. He actually doesn't smell, which makes me hate him more. Dylan's so cocky he drives me crazy.

"Are you jealous, princess?" He moves to stand in front of me. My jaw drops at his insinuation. Jealous of what? I'd never want his bearded ass.

I poke my finger in his strong, well defined, tattooed chest. He's like walking sex right now. "Let's get one thing straight right now. We will not talk about my sex life and I don't care to know about yours. That's final," I say with venom.

"God, I have a hard-on right now." He laughs. I punch him in his arm and get off on his floor.

"Ouch!"

"You probably do get off on this don't you, you Neanderthal." Swinging my purse back over my shoulder, it grazes him and he lets out an "Oof." We head back to his apartment/office. I was so tempted to check to see if he was hard. I smile to myself, because I didn't give him the satisfaction. One point for Team Pink!

"Okay, how can I be a hipster and a Neanderthal?" He gives me a side glance as he opens the door to his apartment.

"You're a Neanderthal trying to be a hipster," I say gruffly. He just sighs at me.

"That makes no sense, Andy." Dylan moves over to the kitchen where the half-naked woman is perched on a barstool eating a banana suggestively. I grimace at her ability to swallow the whole thing in one go. Damn, she has skills. I have a high gag reflex. "Babe, I gotta work now. I'll walk you out." Smooth, very smooth. She doesn't even realize she's getting the boot. She follows him to what I figure is his bedroom.

I'm left alone in his space. It's huge. This would be a great office, if not for the big screen TV, couch, and beanbag chair in the corner. He has windows all on one side that look out over the city. Chicago looks great from here. I spot a desk near one of the windows, with a lamp and some paperwork already piled on top. I walk to the desk and notice he does already have work for me.

The woman walks out of Dylan's room all dressed in a slinky dress. He follows her to the door. He has a pair of jeans and a black Smashing Pumpkins shirt on today. I hate the Smashing Pumpkins. The lead singer's voice sounds like a goat crying. He gives her a quick kiss at the door and shoos her out, oblivious to the dismissal she just received. What a jerk. Looking back to the desk, I notice something . . . there's only one.

"Are you ready to get down to business?" Dylan says as he grabs a box of Frosted Flakes cereal.

"So, there's just one desk." I motion to the one behind me.

"Yeah, I don't need one." He takes a handful of cereal and munches on it while simultaneously chugging a carton of milk. He's like a child, a big man-child. He's also barefoot and kind of sexy like that. Wait, no he's not sexy. He's a Neanderthal. I go back over to the desk and look over the paperwork. Everything seems to be in order. I notice a few things though.

"Dylan, these are some of our clients at Johnson and Banks."

"Yes, princess, they are." He doesn't offer up more than that. This sounds fishy.

"Are you working for the new company?" I start to pace the floor in front of the desk. He's relaxed at a barstool two fisting his breakfast.

"In a way, but I work for myself. Whatever it is you're thinking, don't. It's completely legal. I can show you the paperwork if you'd like." He seems annoyed. Dylan's a smart guy and I know he's intelligent enough not to do anything illegal. I still nod my head. He huffs and picks up a piece of paper under one of the many files on the desk. "Here. Just think of me as an independent contractor for them."

The document says the name of the new company, P. Revere Accounting Firm. Dylan Ryder is listed on the forms and he seems to be working for the new company but not under anyone. Everything seems to be in order.

"Okay, what would you like me to do first? Oh, and one of my conditions was that I would have my own office away from you. I'm basically on top of you here."

"Yeah, you are."

Rolling my eyes, I set my purse down next to the desk.

4

"Dylan, this contract needs to be signed and you have to have a form for this. Oh, and where's my insurance card?"

Dylan pauses his Halo videogame and saunters over to my desk. He signs the document and places it on top of the massive stack. "Your insurance card is in the mail. You should get it by Friday." He smiles and returns to the couch.

"Okay, um, I'm gonna need help bringing up my office supplies. There's a lot. I left the boxes with your doorman this morning." I move to stand in front of him, when I hear his player die in the game. He sneers at me.

"All right." He gets up and puts on his shoes, then stops suddenly. "Wait a minute. You're not doing what I think you are, are you?"

"What do you mean?" Stopping near the doorway, I turn to look at him. I have no idea what he's talking about.

"I don't want a bunch of your frilly, pink, flowery shit in my apartment." The nerve of this asshole!

"Rule three, I need my office supplies in order to do my job." A smug smile graces my face. I hold the front door open for him. This is a non-negotiable issue. My supplies are a necessity to do my job. He's just going to have to deal with my pink shit.

Dylan runs his hand down his face as he groans. "Shit. Motherfucker, flowery shit." He places his hands on his hips and then points to my desk. "All that pink shit stays in that corner, princess, no bleeding anywhere else like the kitchen or bathroom, got it?" Dylan sounds so stern. It's kind of turning me on.

"I just had my period, so we're good." Internally I high five myself for making him uncomfortable. I think I'm going to like this job after all.

"God, Andy. I do not want to know that crap." He rubs at his temples. "We are not girlfriends watching *Golden Girls* while putting oatmeal face masks on. This is business and there will be no talk about that . . . at all, EVER." I smile and open the door for him. He stalks over and points in my face like he's about to say something and then resigns to the elevator. Team Pink: two, Smashing Pumpkins Loser: zero.

We finally get down to business after moving in all my supplies. Dylan's still dressed in his jeans and T-shirt. This will definitely be a different work environment. I have to say he looks just as sexy filling out those dumb band shirts as he does a dress shirt. I mean if I'm stuck with him day in and day out, I can at least appreciate the view. After I have everything in order and where I want it, I turn to him. He's sitting on the couch playing video games. I watch for a little while. "Top left," I say.

"Wha?" The shooter in the videogame takes him out. "Damn it, Andy. I was on a fucking killing spree." He lobs his controller on the coffee table and gets up. "I'm going to make some calls." The bearded monster slithers to his natural habitat, his bedroom, and shuts the door. What's a girl to do when all her work is done? I tap my fingers on the table itching to snag his controller. Fuck it. I'll shatter his killing spree.

I move to the couch and sit on the black leather. Everything is black in here. I haven't seen his comforter in his bedroom yet, but I bet that's black as well. Not that I would ever want to go in there. I grab the controller and hit continue. I wait to join a group and then it's on like Donkey Kong. By the time Dylan comes out of his room, I've obliterated his killing spree and ranked him up.

His phone dangles in his hand to his side. He's completely speechless. I like this Dylan. I giggle to myself.

"What the hell? You play Halo? Please don't tell me this was your first time playing." He collapses on the couch next to me, completely gobsmacked.

"What? Oh yeah, I've never played before." I try and hold in my laughter when I see his jaw drop. "I'm just fucking with you. Halo is my favorite game. Well, besides the old-school games."

"Old-school games?" He looks from the TV to me. See Neanderthal, there is more to me than meets the eye.

"Yeah, I still have my old N64 and SNES." He slides down off the couch onto his knees next to me.

"Marry me." Laughing, I push his shoulder. He falls back on his ass near the coffee table. "How did you get into gaming?" Wow. He actually seems impressed. This is a new turn of events. He's always quick to pigeon hole me. I'm busting out of this cage.

"I was an only child. My dad gave me video games to keep me preoccupied. It worked." I rub my stomach because it's lunchtime and I'm getting hungry. Walking over to his kitchen, I checkout his refrigerator. Typical guy, has nothing in there but cheese and sodas. I turn to look at him but he's right behind me. It startles me but I don't let on. "So, what about those free lunches you mentioned?" I give him a big smile and he returns it. I think he's starting to realize that we have more in common than he originally thought.

"I can make a mean grilled cheese sandwich." He grabs the loaf of bread on the counter.

"Okay, I'm not picky. Sounds good. Do you need any help?" I stand next to him.

"The princess is willing to make her own lunch? This I gotta see." He steps aside and waves his hand. Maybe we haven't progressed as much as I thought.

"What's with all this princess crap you dish out on the regular? Is it the clothes I wear or something? I don't think I give off a superiority vibe." I make myself comfortable in his kitchen. I pop the bread in his toaster and go to grab the butter out of the fridge. The whole time Dylan just studies me as I work.

"Um, don't you need a skillet or something?" He crosses his arms and leans against the counter. It's weird being in his apartment, but I don't feel nervous or unwelcome, even though he's giving me shit again.

"No, I'm ravenous. I need this cheese in my belly now." He squints his eyes, trying to figure out what I'm going to do next. The toast pops out. I slather butter on it. I place some cheese on one side and then pop it in the microwave to melt it a little. When I take it out of the microwave, I lay the other piece of toast on top to make my sandwich. I cut the slice in half and offer him the plate.

"Holy shit. It took you like three minutes to make a grilled cheese sandwich. That must be some kind of record. You're like a wizard." He takes a massive bite and moans. I didn't realize microwaving a sandwich could be seen as magical but I'll take it.

"I just have my own way of doing things, I guess." I make my own sandwich. His eyes are glued to my every move, as if I'm some magical unicorn. "It's not that original. I'm sure lots of college students make grilled cheese like that." Buttering my toast, I lay the cheese on top.

"It's not just the way you make your grilled cheese. It's the way you move in the kitchen. You have these little quirks that I'm sure you're not even aware of." He gruffs a little at his comment, like he's said too much. Dylan attacks his sandwich. I don't know what he's talking about. I stare at him, bewildered. He rolls his eyes at me and finishes his bite. "I shouldn't have said anything."

"No, come on. I want to know what you mean by the

way I move around in the kitchen." I copy his stance and start to eat my grilled cheese. We're both standing in the kitchen eating sandwiches together. This is cozy.

Dylan sets his plate down since he's finished and grabs the counter behind him. "You sway and almost dance around the kitchen. That's the only way I can explain it. The way you pass things from one hand to the other. The way you reach and stretch for things, it's like a ballet. You put the perfect amount of butter on the toast. You twisted the loaf of bread closed by twirling it in front of you."

Was he watching me that closely? I guess I don't think about the way I do things. I just do them. I've never thought of myself as graceful. I don't really know what to say. That was really sweet. I stare at him, not understanding these emotions bubbling up.

"Just forget it. Let's talk about something else. Do you need any other office supplies?"

Standing there for a minute, I mull over what Dylan just said. It's a weird comment to make about the way someone moves around the kitchen, who notices that? It may have changed how I see him a little. He seems embarrassed that he spoke about it. I feel we are making progress toward a better working relationship. At least he can say something nice for a change.

Dylan moves over to my desk, looks it over and shakes his head. "It's all pink. What is it with you and pink? You asked earlier why I call you princess, it's because of all this." He waves his hand around my desk.

"What can I say? It makes me happy. I work better when everything looks pretty and is organized."

"I bet your home is like this too, isn't it, all pink and frilly?" He chuckles to himself. I don't really take offense though because it's true. I take another bite of my sandwich and sit down at my desk. I believe we're actually taking the time to get to know one another now.

"Well, it was no shocker that your whole apartment is black, Prince of Darkness." I smile up at him. He looks around as if he didn't notice that his place is monochrome. His eyes settle on me after a moment and he gives me this look. I don't even know how to describe it. It's like he's seeing me for the first time, maybe in a new light. And just like that it's gone.

"I gotta go run an errand. I'll be back before five." He grabs his leather jacket on the way out the door. Huh, I wonder what the hell that was about. I finish my sandwich and continue getting folders together and sorted.

At 4:55, Dylan finally graces me with his presence. There's a quick, "Hi" and then a "See ya, tomorrow." I'm almost pushed out the door. That has got to be the weirdest first day of work ever.

5

The work week passes quickly, mostly because Dylan gives me a lot of space. He's avoiding me. It's weird. I welcome the quiet and the time to work in his big open space. Although, I debate whether I should ask him if I can bring my pet to work. It's been quite lonely with him barricaded in his bedroom. He handles all the calls, so I don't have anyone to talk to unless I go out and get lunch somewhere and then it's just giving my order.

Standing up from my desk, I move to his bedroom door, feeling like I'm impeding on his privacy. Softly, I knock on the door. The bed squeaks and there's shuffling then Dylan's head pops out. He just stares at me, like I might bite him.

"So, I was wondering if I could bring my little pet to work tomorrow? She's potty trained and she won't be in the way. I promise. I'm just used to a little more social interaction than this." I look down at my feet, a little ashamed that I'm letting him know I'm lonely. Glancing back up, I give him my puppy dog eyes. Maybe it will help. He has a phone tucked to his chest, like it's on hold.

He seems to debate my question rather quickly. "It doesn't chew on stuff, does it?" he whispers.

"Oh, no. She's perfectly harmless." I smile big. Dylan seems to be in a hurry to get back on the phone.

"Fine, but keep her out of my way. This is a work environment, after all." He shuts the door quickly. "Yeah, Sam I'm still here." His voice moves away from the door. I hop a little at my excitement. Birdie is coming to work with me! Maybe this job does have its perks! I've always wanted to bring my pet to work. I feel bad about leaving her home all day. She'll be so excited.

The next day, I walk Birdie up to his apartment and knock as usual. There hasn't been an incident like that first day. He's been a man of his word, so far anyway. I wait patiently for him to open the door. He unlocks it, and without a backward glance, turns away from the door. He's already on the phone. Birdie follows me in to my desk.

"Yeah, okay. I got it. Sounds good. Thanks, Sam." Dylan turns around from his phone call and drops the phone on the floor. "What the hell is that?" He points toward my pet with a shocked expression.

I motion to Birdie. "Oh, this is the pet I asked to bring to work yesterday, remember? This is Birdie. See, she's sweet." My little piglet makes her way over to Dylan and nudges his leg. When I moved from Alabama, Birdie had to come with me. I couldn't leave her at home with my dad. He hardly took care of me. He threatened to turn her into bacon for years. He's a cold human being. I'm so glad I brought her. It's been lonely in the city. I don't have many friends but my pig keeps me company.

"Oh my God. You have a pet pig. I should have known you'd have something pink. Jesus, Andy, I can't have a pig in my apartment. How do you have a pig in your apartment?" He makes no move to touch her, but he lets her rub all over him. She's friendly to everyone, even if they are bearded monsters that go back on their word.

"My landlord doesn't really know about her. But, she's just like a dog. She's very domesticated. In fact, some people believe pigs are more intelligent than dogs." I bend down to call Birdie to me. She trots on over and rolls on her back so I can rub her belly. She makes the most adorable little rooting sound.

"When you said pet I was thinking of some shelter dog, not a pig. Why couldn't you just have a normal pet? And who the hell names a pig Birdie?" He's exasperated with me.

Stomping my foot like a two-year-old, I try to stop my eyes from tearing up. I knew he'd be an asshole about it. I should just expect this kind of behavior from him. "Fine, I'll just take her back home then." I move to the door, but Dylan rushes in front of me. I hang my head down so he can't see the tears running down my cheeks. I don't know why this made me so upset. Either it's the fact that he thinks I'm weird, or that he wishes I were normal? Then he does something I'd never expect. Dylan places his finger under my chin to raise my head. The look he gives me is one of concern and remorse.

"I'm sorry, Andy. I was just a little surprised at the

situation. I didn't mean to hurt your feelings. Birdie can stay." He removes his fingers from my chin and crouches down to Birdie. Dylan pats her on the back and she squeals at him, as if she knows he said she could stay. "Does she need a water bowl or anything?" I sniff and wipe my nose on the back of my hand. I hold up the pink tote I brought. It has a few of Birdie's toys, her water bowl, snacks, treats, and food. He looks in the bag and smiles. "Even her toys are pink." I never thought I'd see Dylan smile at something pink.

I get over my speechlessness. "Thank you." Birdie immediately digs out her favorite toy. It's a Peppa Pig that squeaks. My little piglet makes herself at home on his rug, in front of the TV with Peppa. I peek at Dylan to make sure that's all right. He rolls his eyes. I can't believe he's allowing her to stay. I'm surprised he didn't give her the boot.

"We good?" Dylan places a hand on my shoulder and squeezes it.

"Yeah," I reply, nodding my head. A warm fuzzy feeling covers my whole body. It's nice when Dylan doesn't treat me like a princess. He's actually baffled me quite a bit since working for him. His apartment is starting to feel like my home away from home, black couch and all. Dylan picks up the phone and moves to the sofa, where I see paperwork sprawled out on the coffee table. He's such a mess. Birdie notices him on the couch and jumps up to sit next to him.

"Uh, Andy?" He holds his hands up, like he's under arrest.

I laugh a little to myself. I want to see how this plays out. "Yeah?"

Dylan lowers his hands and Birdie nudges him with her nose. His hand falls on top of her head. He pets her timidly. Everyone loves Birdie; there's no way anyone can resist her charms. I smile at the adorable sight. This big, burly, tattooed man petting my cute pink pig. I'm getting that warm fuzzy feeling again.

"Never mind," he huffs. Sucker.

The day goes by quickly. Before I know it, it's time for Birdie and me to leave. My piglet's been a permanent fixture at Dylan's side. The bearded monster seems to embrace it. He loves on her when he thinks I'm not looking. It's the cutest thing I've ever seen.

Dylan seems a little sad to see us head out. He must get lonely too. Wait, no he's probably going to go out and land a chick, or whatever they call it. Unless he's still seeing that girl I met on my first day. She was pretty, even if she had just woken up. I feel a little jealous. I don't know why. It's not like I want to be with Dylan in that way. I mean my boss is very attractive, especially when he's being nice. I think back to when he said I could keep Birdie. My heart flutters. *Stop that heart.* He's a Prince of Darkness, bearded hipster . . . that thinks I move like a ballerina in the kitchen. I still can't get over his unusual but sweet comment.

I turn to say goodbye to Dylan. His face looks solemn. I'm almost tempted to give him a hug and a kiss on the cheek. Birdie and I just stand there at his door. Dylan stares back.

"Is something wrong, Andy?" I love how he says my name, even if he's a gruff Neanderthal. Swiftly, I walk over and give him a hug, in a way of thanks for letting me bring Birdie to work. As I wrap my arms around his waist, he tenses up. He drops his head back and closes his eyes. It's like it's physically painful to touch me. What the hell? His arms are stiff at his sides and his hands are in fists. I let go of him, shocked by his reaction to my hug. He finally lets out the breath he's been holding.

I push my hair back behind my ear and play with my earring. "Umm, I just wanted to say thanks for letting me bring Birdie to work." I pick up Birdie and close the door behind me. I didn't realize I repulsed him so much. Who gives that kind of reaction to a hug? Birdie snuggles in my arms. I'm glad I at least have some wanted attention.

6

We all settle into a routine. Before I know it, it's been a month. I've received two paychecks. They are everything he said they'd be and more. I'm happy to come to work for him every day. It seems business has picked up too. Our little firm is doing great. Birdie even has a small bed near my desk. There are a few of my mugs in his kitchen. I even talked him into having some peach hand wash in his bathroom. It smells divine. Maybe I can convince him to get some softer hand towels?

I managed to snoop in his bedroom one day and confirm his comforter is black. I wasn't snooping initially, I was searching for a document I was missing. Then I happened to have the great idea of looking around and I found his condom stash in his side table drawer, along with a vibrator. What does a guy do with a vibrator? I don't think I want to know. *Or maybe I do. No, Andy. He's a bearded monster and your boss. Cool your heels, girl.*

Dylan was right. He doesn't smell like your typical, natural hipster. My boss' clothes smell very nice and clean. His closet is even somewhat organized. Then Birdie had to ruin my fun and snuggle on his bed. She obviously thinks he smells good too.

I've spoken to Cindy off and on; she finally managed to get another job. It's closer to her home, but it doesn't pay as well as her old position. She's getting by, but barely. I'm keeping my eye out for any positions available in the city for her. So far, there have been no leads.

It's Friday, and I'm a little sad I'm not going to see Dylan tomorrow. I'm comfortable here in his apartment. Who would have thought? I'm typing out an e-mail when he strolls through the front door. "Hey, Andy. I've got good news." I make my way over to him. Dylan pulls out a bottle of water, my idea by the way. "I landed that big client. I think we can expand, hire a few new staff and move to an actual office space."

Sadness pulls in my stomach. This should be good news. I guess I've become too comfortable with being in his apartment. It's been nice with just the two of us working together. "That's great news, Dylan." I try to put on a good face.

He bends down and pets Birdie. "Birdie is welcome in the new office, of course. She's become a bit of our mascot. Let's celebrate. We can go out on the town and have a nice dinner, what do you say?" I could use a drink right now. I'm still trying to understand this conflicting feeling I have about expanding the business. I probably shouldn't be drinking around my boss. Oh, who am I kidding, it's just Dylan.

"Great! Let me just grab my purse." Pondering the move as I gather my things, I think about how I like it here and how we do things. I like that it's just him and I. We have a system set in place here. Moving from another job; I need routine and I actually like my desk here. Feeling a bit melancholy over this, I try not to let it show.

"Sorry, Birdie girl, I don't think where we are going pigs are welcome. I'll bring you some scraps." Dylan rubs behind her ear and she's putty in his hands. She's fallen for his bearded charms. "I'm just going to change real quick." He heads to his bedroom, while I make sure Birdie has enough food and water. At my desk, I turn off my computer and sit down. Struggling with the idea of not being here much longer, I think of Cindy. She could work with Dylan. She'd love it. He pays really well and the benefits are great. Maybe this isn't as bad as I thought. I guess I'm just going to miss the comradery we have. Maybe I'm developing feelings for the schmuck. Damn.

Birdie's practically already asleep in her bed by the time Dylan comes out. "Wow. I think I need to go home and change." He's wearing a button-up blue shirt with the sleeves rolled up and some dark black dress slacks. His hair is combed back and it looks like he's trimmed his beard a little. Dylan looks hot. I get a tingling feeling between my legs. I might need to slap myself. I can't believe I'm feeling attracted to him. He smirks at me. Bastard.

"Okay, we're stopping by my place. It's close." Leading the way to the door, he grabs his jacket and we walk out.

"Okay, admit it. I'm right. Everything is pink." Dylan's waiting in my living room while I change. I decided to go with my red dress and change it up. I've been dying to have a place to wear this baby. Plus, I want him checking me out in this, make him pay for my gawking at his apartment.

"My TV isn't pink. Or my coffee table, or my two accent chairs." I smile at his huff from the other room.

"Okay, everything except three things are pink." He laughs. I slip on my dress and walk to the living room. He's checking out my movie collection. He calls out, thinking I'm still in the bathroom. "You like *Die Hard*?"

"Yippie-Ki-Yay, motherfucker!" He turns swiftly to face me. His jaw drops, and I know I chose the right dress. He arranges himself through the pockets of his slacks. "Also, you haven't seen my sleeping area." My studio apartment is large enough that I have a large wall unit breaking up the room. Grabbing my clutch, I wait at the door for him. Dylan's still ogling me. He clears his throat and rubs the back of his neck, shaking it off. Then he places his hand on my lower back as we walk out the door. This feels like we are on a date. I don't know how I feel about that.

"So, where are we going? I'm dying for a hamburger. I hope this place has hamburgers." He turns to me, shock on his face.

"You want a hamburger? I was going to take you to this

French restaurant downtown, but your idea sounds better. Come on, I know just the place." He grabs my hand, leads me to his car and opens the door for me. Okay, this definitely feels like a date. He seemed surprised I wanted a hamburger. He must think I'm some diva, and I only eat where there are waiters or something. I could totally go for a McDonald's cheeseburger right now.

On the way there, we speak briefly about the expansion. He's aching to get an office space. He hates being holed up in his apartment all the time. I guess we have opposite opinions on that matter.

We park at a dive bar called Hops. It looks a little seedy, but fun. "I never in a million years thought I'd bring you here, but this place has the best burgers in all of Chicago."

"Let's go, then." I open my door and step out. He's right there to lead me into the bar. I also didn't expect this Neanderthal to act like a gentleman. Sad to say, most guys these days don't open doors it seems. Maybe it's just the guys I tend to date.

Hops is exactly what I thought it would be. There are peanut shells on the floor and pints of beer scattered throughout the tabletops. It's quant and quiet. I love it. We are seated immediately. Dylan hands the menus back to the waitress. "We already know what we want. Two burgers and fries, please."

"What drinks?" The waitress looks up from her notepad. We finish our order and she heads back to the kitchen. It's a little awkward. I don't really know what to talk about. We're usually fighting or working. This is new territory.

"They have a condiment bar, where you can add cheese and pickles, customize your burger the way you want. I love this place." Dylan has a bit of a glow and I can't help feeling happy to be here with him. This is a new side of Dylan Ryder. I think he's finally warmed up to me. I don't want to say anything though and ruin what we have going.

Honestly, I'm a little confused about my feelings for him right now. I was dead set on leaving him in the shmuck category, but he's proven to me that he's a decent guy. He treats Birdie like a princess. He's even stopped calling me princess. It wouldn't really bother me anymore if he called me that, though.

There's no denying that he's hot tonight. I may have worn my red lingerie under this dress in hopes he would see it. God, I'm so confused. There's no chance in hell that would happen. Plus, he's my boss. *Dylan is your boss, Andy!*

You can tell he'd be great in bed, though. I've never had great in bed. All of my exes were interested in getting off as quickly as possible and didn't worry about me in the process. They never seemed concerned I didn't come, selfish jerks.

"What are you thinking about, Andy? Your cheeks are flushed." His hands are folded in front of him, his large hands. I don't know why that turns me on. It's not like I thought about hands before. Maybe because I'm wondering what he can do with them.

"Nothing, this place is nice. I can't wait to dig into my burger." The bearded monster smiles a knowing smile. I give him a little scowl and he laughs at me.

"You're cute when you get mad." What? Dylan clears his throat and looks away.

He changes the subject quickly back to work. Maybe that was a slip of the tongue. Soon we get our drinks, and he takes a big gulp from his pint. His beard pulls away from the cup. A few of his whiskers have froth clinging to them. Dylan notices me looking at his mouth. He licks off the froth and I clench my thighs together.

"You should see me when I'm pissed." I smile at him and take a drink of my Long Island ice tea.

"I have, it's hot." He runs his hands down his beard and I follow the motion. What the hell is happening. Is it hot in here? Why is he being so complimentary? I don't know how to react to this new Dylan. His light brown eyes roam over me. Fuck.

"I need to use the restroom." I rise up quickly and make my way to the back of the bar. After washing my hands, I check myself in the mirror. I am a little flushed. God, what is he doing to me? I grab a paper towel and wet it under the faucet. Ringing it out, I place it on the back of my neck. *Oh, that feels good.* After I cool off a little, I throw the paper towel in the trash. Back at the table, I sit across from Dylan. He's really hot sitting here drinking a pint. He looks over my face and then glances down at my chest. His eyes stay there for a while. "Geez, Dylan, could you be any more obvious?"

"Sorry, Andy. You have a drop of water running down

between your breasts. I'm only human." He points at my cleavage. I look down and sure enough, there is a water droplet that seems to have run from my neck to the space between my boobs. I wipe it up quickly. He's still staring. Dylan mumbles "Fuck" under his breath, as he rubs his eyes with the palms of his hands. That was an irritated response. They're only boobs. It's not like I was flashing him. What is up with him tonight? He's running hot and then cold. I have no idea where I stand with the Neanderthal.

The waitress drops our burgers in front of us. "Thank God." The waitress looks confused at Dylan. "I'm just really hungry." The way he says hungry makes me shiver. What is going on at this table? I'm going to eat quickly so we can get out of here and in the fresh air. There's something in the water here.

We mostly stick to conversation about work and Birdie. The awkward moment is thankfully forgotten and when we leave the restaurant, we're laughing about Birdie's gas habits. "Oh my God, that one was so bad. I have no idea what she ate that day."

"It was probably one of those KFC biscuits. She goes crazy over those." Dylan opens the car door for me and waits for me to get in before getting behind the wheel and pulling out of the parking lot. "I'm glad you liked that place. I'd never picture you there. This sounds a little juvenile, but do you want to come over to my place and play some video games?"

I laugh at his question. "You just want me to rank you up again." He nods his head enthusiastically. "Okay, under one condition." His eyebrows perk up and he waits for my condition. "I get to bring my pink radio into the office next week so I can listen to music."

"Ugh, come on. You probably listen to . . . I don't know Cindy Lauper and shit." He turns onto his street.

"Yes, I do like Cindy Lauper and shit, but I also like Depeche Mode, The Cure, Billy Idol, The Weeknd, The 1975, Bastille. I could go on." This is what I'm talking about. He makes assumptions because of the way I dress and decorate. I can only like pop songs because I dress preppy. No, I can be just as dark as the next person.

"You like The Cure? You gave me shit about my shirt forever, and you like them? Name a song."

"'Feels Like Heaven,'" I say smugly. On casual days at work he would always wear that shirt. I did always give him crap about it because, well, he got on my nerves and I knew it bothered him.

He shakes his head as he pulls into his parking spot. "Every girl knows 'Feels Like Heaven.'"

I step to get out. "'Friday I'm in Love,' 'Love Song,' 'Pictures of You,' 'Let's go to Bed.'"

"What?" His head snaps back to me. Dylan stops at the elevator.

"The song, 'Let's go to Bed.'" What did he think, that I was propositioning him? As if!

"Oh yeah, okay. Okay. Fine. I'll let you bring your pink radio to the office, on a probationary period only though."

"Deal." I hold my hand out to him and he shakes it lightly.

I take off my shoes when we get to his apartment and

lie down on my stomach, waiting for the game to boot up. Dylan follows my lead and hands me a controller.

7

"This is so weird." I know what he means, but sometimes the weirdest things are the most fun. I'm able to rank him up over a couple of hours. He's playing as a guest, which makes me giggle. I give him some of my tips. Dylan tells me his favorite maps. We start to play against each other, which is the most fun. "I can't believe that cheap sniper shot you just did."

I scoff. "How is that cheap? Deal with it, baby. You can't handle my gaming skills." I polish off my fingernails on my shoulder. I'm awesome at this game. I love it when people underestimate me. My kills streak speaks for itself.

"You talk a big game for a girl." Dylan sits up and tosses his controller in front of him.

"Well, this girl just beat your ass." His jaw drops. I snicker at him, and sit up, leaving my controller on the floor. He gets this serious look on his face and then he grabs my face. His lips encompass mine and I'm in bearded kiss bliss. I close my eyes and feel his tongue probing my mouth. Slowly, I open my mouth as his beard tickles my face. I'm unsure what's going on. *Am I seriously French kissing Dylan Ryder right now?*

My lips and tongue are acting of their own accord, playing with his mouth. His very sexy, hot mouth. He tastes really good, like Fruity Pebbles or some cereal. He was munching on it while we were playing. I might have to take up eating cereal in the mornings . . . or snacks or just kissing him. His beard is soft and tickles, it's just making me hotter. Needing some friction, I move over and straddle his lap. He gasps when I sit on top of him. I'm not ashamed of my forwardness; I never have been. It seems to surprise him though. His hand moves from my head to my ass, moving me against him. His very hard cock rubs against my core. We slide against each other like we're in heat. I'm dry humping my boss.

Obviously, I'm not really thinking. I'm only feeling how good his body feels against mine. Gasping for breath, I break from his face.

"Andy." That right there is the sexiest sound I've ever heard in my life. My head drops back as he kisses along my neck down to my breasts. Are we really taking this to a place of no return? Will this change everything?

"Dylan." Except my outburst sounds more like a question. I'm trying to figure out how I got into this position. Birdie comes over to see what the commotion is all about and tries to nuzzle between us. Dylan is having none of that. He rises up with me in his arms and my legs wrap around his waist. My dress rides up as he cups my ass.

Dylan walks me into his bedroom. I'm in the Prince of Darkness' cave. He closes his bedroom door with his foot and places me on his bed. It's dark and I'm not talking about the colors. The only light is coming from his closet. A shadow is cast across his face, it makes him look dark and dangerous. Dylan stares at me for a minute. I'm trying to breathe. His hair falls partially in his eyes. God, he's hot. His turned-on face is melting my panties off my body.

Dylan stands at the end of the bed and removes his shirt. There are all his tattoos on display. He looks like bad decisions. I can't wait to see what the rest of him looks like. His six pack is mostly bare of ink. I wonder if he has any hidden under his pants? He's just staring back at me. I've just been lying here staring at his amazing physique, unashamed.

"Do you have any idea how bad I've wanted you in my bed?" Shaking my head, I'm not able to say a single word. I thought he disliked me. I'm not even sure if he likes me now. We're so different. Maybe we're going to have angry sex. Wow, I wonder what that would be like. He'd probably pound me through his bed to the floor. Sounds divine. I need a good pounding. I've had quite the dry spell.

His chest is rising and falling quickly. I gaze down his body, where his slacks are hanging off his hips. He has that V. It makes me want to lick up and down it. His stomach is taut. I knew he was muscular under his dress shirts but this is unreal. I might be drooling and I don't care if he catches me gawking. Pulling the hem of my dress down, I don't want him to see how wet I am. I want him bad. I want to know what he can do with my body. "Pull up your dress for me. I want to see those panties." Whoa. Dylan's eyes are intense.

Yes, sir.

Scrunching the material in my grasp, I slowly raise it up. He unbuckles his belt and keeps his eyes on the slow rise of my dress. Dylan's boxers drop with his pants when my dress hits my wet, red panties. His cock is even bigger than it felt, if that's possible. It looks angry and ready to pound into me. In anticipation, I slowly remove my dress for him as he strokes his hard cock. I grip the blanket and watch him pleasure himself. I've never seen a guy stroke it in front of me before. It's hot. I'm almost tempted to touch myself too. His tattooed arms strain against the pleasure, his face in deep concentration. I moan. Dylan's eyes light up. He bends over still holding his cock, and with his teeth he starts to pull my panties down my quivering legs. How did I get from playing video games to lying naked in Dylan Ryder's bed? He's got some sexy magic.

Dylan's hand comes up and removes my panties the rest of the way. Then his face nuzzles my bare pussy. His beard brushes against my mound, it tickles, and makes me wet with need. "I knew you'd smell good." He gives it a sweet kiss, which makes me whimper. "You want me to fuck this pussy?" I'm white knuckling his comforter as I nod my head. I don't trust myself with words right now. I might say something like, I love you, huge dick, or ketchup.

Who knows? One thing is for sure, I want him to pound me with his huge dick.

"Tell me, Andy. Tell me you want my cock fucking you until you come. I want to hear it from those sweet, pouty lips."

Closing my eyes, I find my voice. "Make me come," I plead. "Please!" I'm begging and I don't care. My body is shuttering, waiting for him to command it with his hands, his body. I open my eyes to see his reaction.

He rubs the side of my thigh. "It's okay, princess. I'll make you come. The question is how many times?" Dylan opens the snap on the front of my bra with one hand, as the other hikes my leg around his waist. My breasts are free, and immediately pebble under the cool air. He hovers over me, taking in my face and chest. "You're so beautiful. I've wanted to put my hands on your body for so long. You drive me fucking insane, Andy." I'm surprised to say the least by his admission. I want to ask him questions but my brain isn't working very well. He dips his head down and kisses down my chest. My hands move to his tattooed shoulders.

Dylan licks around one nipple and then moves to the other. His hand caresses down my body until he reaches my mound. I gasp as strong fingers slide between my folds and rub my wetness around. He moans against my breast. Then it's my turn to moan, when his finger enters me slowly. My knees rise up and I open my legs wider for him.

"Fuck. Yes, Andy. Open that pussy for me." I've never had a lover talk during sex, let alone talk dirty. It turns me on even more. I clutch his head and moan into his hair.

Dylan is stroking me a little faster now. His thumb has moved to play with my clit and just like that, I'm having my first orgasm with him. I throw my head back and scratch at his back. I have no control over where this orgasm goes. It's so intense; more than any I've ever had before.

"Oh my God, Dylan," I whisper after my orgasm has subsided a little. My pussy is still humming and my whole body is quivering. I feel so weak but energized at the same time.

"Mmmm, I love the way you sigh my name after you come." He kisses me intensely with his tongue and then pulls quickly away. "One." Dylan moves off the bed and stands. He grabs my ankles and pulls my legs across the bed until my butt is on the edge. He kneels between my legs.

"Dylan!" I push my hands between my legs to cover my mound. He bats them away.

"Don't tell me no one has tipped this velvet." Slowly, I shake my head. "Oh baby, you've been with boys. Don't worry, princess. Here's number two." Dylan kisses the apex of my thighs before moving to my slit. I'm breathlessly watching his sexy face between my legs. My most private part is open for inspection. Dylan gives me one slow lick, tickling my clit. I gasp and run my fingers through his hair. His head rocks side to side between my thighs. Closing my eyes, I just feel his tongue, mouth, and beard on the most delicate part of me. It's so erotic. He spreads my thighs farther apart when I start to clench my legs. I shout and thrash my head side to side before crashing beautifully apart on his tongue.

Things are all jumbled in my head right now, but one thing stands out. Dylan said he never goes down on one-night stands. I don't know what's going to happen after this or if we can still work together, but I take comfort in the fact he doesn't see me as just another hookup.

Dylan licks up from my navel trailing between my breasts, stopping to kiss each nipple. He reaches my mouth and I taste my release on his tongue. It's heady. I grip the back of his neck and hold him to my mouth. He presses his pelvis against mine and his hard cock rubs against my folds. I pull at Dylan's back so that he lies on top of me. "I'm ready for number three, Mr. Ryder." I pull out the drawer where his condoms are and pull one out. His eyebrows go up and then he smirks. He doesn't say anything, just watches me.

Opening the wrapper, I roll it on him. Dylan has a quick intake of breath when I grab him at his base. "That's right, baby. Guide me in. Let me feel how tight you are inside." I rub his head against my entrance while playing with his sack. "Fuck. Touch me just like that." He gives me a kiss and pushes inside me to the hilt. "Oh, fuck." I hear him gulp as I gasp. I'm stretched to the max and he's stilled inside me. I grab his face so I can look at him as he slowly pulls out and enters me again. We both moan.

I've never felt a connection like this with someone during sex. I'm so turned on. He's touching me in all these unbelievable ways. I can't keep my hands off his taut muscular body. His tattoos are a stark contrast to my untouched skin. It makes me feel delicate. He hovers over me, caging me in. I feel so safe with him, like nothing can touch me except him.

Dylan rests his forehead against mine as he slowly picks up the pace. His breath exhales across my face and mine hitches. I never want this feeling to end. Dylan has a light sheen of sweat on his chest. His hair is a little damp at his hairline and I can't help running my hand through it. He looks so beautiful on top of me. My hands run down from his head to grab his neck. "Kiss me," I command. I want this image engrained in my mind forever.

He groans against my lips, still pumping rhythmically in and out of me. Dylan has one hand braced next to my head and the other gripping my hip. Every few pumps he looks down to where we connect. His mouth opens and closes with his ministrations. Every move, exhale, caress he administers turns me on. Dylan oozes sex.

"I'm going to give it to you, Andy." He kisses my temple, a loving gesture and then he's off, pumping hard against my pelvis. He growls as I claw down his back. "Three," Dylan whispers. His hand slides between us. He rubs my clit and I hit that familiar plateau with him. My body goes limp as my orgasm carries on and on. The only part of my body I have control over is my face which is making a silent O. He's just fucking my body, taking it over completely. I lose my hearing for a moment and then I can hear myself screaming his name.

Dylan removes his hands from my wrists. Apparently, at some point he restrained me during my orgasm. He collapses on top of me. I rub his back and he breathes deeply.

"Did you?" I ask.

He chuckles a little in my neck and rolls over. "Yeah, sweetheart. I did."

Damn it. I missed his come face. Shit.

8

"That was unplanned. This isn't going to be weird is it?" Dylan asks. We're both lying in his bed post-coitus under the comforter. I'm debating whether I should just leave or wait for this to get more awkward.

"Have you ever noticed when someone asks if it's gonna get weird, it does regardless?" Dylan chuckles at my comment. He puts his hands behind his head. I can't see his face from the corner of my eye anymore.

"I tried really hard not to like you, Andy, but you're so full of surprises. It was inevitable. You're like this elf-like being with a pink shire who listens to The Cure, watches *Die Hard*, and beats my ass at Halo. All your pink shit drives me crazy and it's infiltrated my apartment. But every time I look at you, I catch myself smiling."

"Did you just *Lord of the Rings* me?" I turn my head toward him. His hands slowly move down from his head. I'm deflecting his comment. I don't really know what to say. I've always liked him even though he drives me insane. Now that I think about it, maybe it was all foreplay?

"Out of all that I said . . . that's what you focus on?" He raises off the bed and leans back on his elbows.

"Well, yeah. The elves are my favorite. I don't know what it is about Thranduil, but he's just hot. Gets me every time." I can't believe he likes me . . . I thought I was just convenient, but for him to actually admit that he likes me. Wow. I need time to process this and get my bearings.

"God, you talking about *Lord of the Rings* gets me fucking hard." Dylan pushes the comforter down and kicks it off the bed. He's on me in two seconds, kissing me fiercely. He flips me over on my stomach pulling my hips toward him. "Here comes number four. Brace yourself against the headboard, baby. This is going to be a pounding." He slaps my ass and I stretch out my hands. I glance back and Dylan's just looking at my ass and caressing it. He bends to kiss one cheek and then sits up to roll a condom on and then he slams into me. My body juts forward.

"Fuck!" I yell and then groan. Turning my head back, I check him out. He looks glorious.

"Yes. You like that? Damn, you're so wet, Andy." Dylan pounds a relentless rhythm against my backside. I've never been in this position before, let alone taken twice in one night. So many firsts for me. Who knew Dylan was a sex god? I mean, he had the rugged don't care vibe and I could picture him knowing what to do in bed, but I didn't think he'd be this good. He's maneuvering my body at just the right angles to bring us the most pleasure. I wonder how many women he's been with?

He slows his ministrations and grips my hips a little lighter. I feel him kiss my back. His beard scruffs against my skin. He's completely changed the mood. Dylan's being softer, sweet. It's a complete one-eighty from where we just were. I don't understand this sudden shift.

"Lie on your side, sweetheart." I look back at him unsure. His eyes are piercing, but tender. After a beat, I move to my side. Dylan shuffles behind me. I suddenly feel his hand between my legs. He lifts my leg back and rests it on his hip. Dylan whispers in my ear, "You're so soft." He exhales against my ear. His hand slides up to cup one of my breasts and then slowly moves down to my pussy. Kisses trickle down my neck as he grips his shaft and rubs it against my opening.

"Tell me you want it, Andy." I can hear the want in his voice and there's nothing I want more in this moment.

"I want you inside me, Dylan," I whisper, rubbing my ass against him. He groans.

Slowly, he enters me. His pace is measured and seductive. I revel in every touch. I can feel every ridge and vein rubbing inside of me, it's different. Even when guys went slow like this in bed, it didn't feel this good. His every exhale at my ear turns me on even more. I sense he's holding back and it's killing him.

I grip the sheets as my orgasm comes out of nowhere and slams into me. I bury my face in the sheets and scream. It's so severe it's like an out of body experience.

"Fuck baby, your pussy is wringing out my cock. Shit."

Dylan grunts, as his pumping becomes irregular. I turn to try and look at his orgasmic face, but he grabs my face and kisses me hard. He pushes my leg to the mattress as he swivels his body, so he's now on top of me and between my legs again. We're making out with our tongues twisting and mingling. This feels so intimate. Dylan finally ceases his kisses and I can breathe again. He stares down at me for a moment and then pushes off.

Dylan moves to go to the bathroom as I lie like a limp noodle. *What the hell just happened here?* I should probably go. I sit up as the bathroom door opens. I know, I must look like a deer in headlights. I don't really know what the protocol for this is. Is this a relationship now? Are we just boinking or was this a one-time thing? He's my boss. This complicates things. I have no idea what he's thinking.

"Hi." He rubs the back of his neck. Dylan looks just as confused as I am.

"Hi." I pull his sheets up to cover my breasts. "I guess I should go." His eyebrows scrunch together. Dylan pulls some boxers on.

"Yeah, I'll just check on Birdie." Before I know it, he's out of the bedroom and I'm in total darkness.

"Ugh!" I fall back on the bed and rub my eyes. This is seriously a clusterfuck. I sit back up and swing my legs out. Picking up the trail of my clothes on the floor, I go to the bathroom to clean up and get dressed. By the time I come out of the bedroom, Dylan is drinking some amber liquid from a tumbler. I play with my earring not knowing where to go from here.

He doesn't say anything. Dylan just keeps glancing between me and the glass he's holding. I really don't understand what's going on. Did I hurt his feelings by suggesting I go? Does he want me to go and is just waiting for me to get my shit together? Forget this. I just need to go home and think about this. Thank God it's the weekend. I have a few days to get my shit together before I have to report back on Monday.

"Congratulations on your new client. I had a nice night." I sound lame. His eyebrows rise up as if he's in disbelief I'm being so obtuse.

Dylan raises his glass up like he's giving a toast. "Congratulations on your four orgasms, princess." He sips the liquid. I feel my face turn red. That bastard! I huff and grab my purse.

"Come on, Birdie. We are leaving." She slowly rises from her bed and saunters toward me. I scoop her up in my arms as Dylan just stays in his spot in the living room. I don't know why he's being such an asshole now. Maybe it was a hate fuck? But he was so gentle the last time.

"You're such an asshole!" He just smiles at me like all is right in the world. I slam the door behind me. The entire walk home, I replay the events of the night over and over again. What could I have done differently? Did I do something wrong or is he just being his usual self? He puts me in knots and drives me crazy. Before I know it, I'm at my building. Birdie is acting a little fidgety. We're finally on my floor and just as I'm pulling out my keys to open my door, I notice my door is already open.

I gasp. It's entirely dark in my apartment except for a

few beams of moonlight from the windows. The outside street lights shine on a few items strewn across the floor. My eyes adjust and I see my apartment has been ransacked. Tears blur my vision and I know I shouldn't be here alone. I place Birdie down as she plows right through the door.

"Birdie!" I sob. Digging in my purse, I grab hold of my cell. I dial the only number I can think of where I can get help. It rings and rings. It goes to voicemail and I hear the dreaded beep. I choke on a cry and hang up. I try calling again. "Please pick up." I can't hear Birdie or anything coming from my apartment. I just hope no one is in there waiting.

The voicemail comes on again. Beep. "Please." I sniffle. "I need help. Someone broke in my apartment and Birdie's gone in there and I don't know what to do." I hear a click.

"Andy? What did you say?"

"Dylan. My apartment is a mess and the door is open and Birdie . . ."

"Andy, get out of there right now. Go down to the front of the building. I'll be there in five minutes. You hear me?"

I sniffle. "Yes."

"Don't go in that apartment. I'm on my way." I can hear him huffing on the phone like he's running. Thank goodness, he's coming. "Stay on the phone with me, so I know you're okay."

"Okay, I'm in front of the building." Three minutes later I see him running to my building. It's the most comforting sight. He doesn't slow down until he's right in front of me. I don't think. I just grab his jacket and cry into his neck. He rubs my shoulders and hugs me tightly.

"It's okay. It's okay, I'm here. I'm so sorry, Andy." He pulls away and grabs my face. He stares down at me and wipes away my tears.

"Birdie," I sob. I grab his wrists, not wanting to let go of him.

"I'll go get her and check out your place." His right hand moves from my face and into his jacket pocket. Dylan pulls out a flashlight.

"Maybe we should call the cops first? What if it's not safe?" I hold on to him tighter. He rubs my cheek.

"I'll be quick. Don't worry. You wait right here. I'll bring Birdie down." Before I can argue, Dylan's going up to my apartment.

I hold my cell phone tightly in my hand, watching the clock. Three minutes and forty-five seconds later I see Dylan holding Birdie in his arms. "Birdie!" He hands her off to me. "Don't you ever run like that again." I kiss her little snout and snuggle her. I feel Dylan's hand on my back, rubbing.

"I turned all the lights on. Some of your stuff was stolen and your apartment is in disarray. You should probably call the cops before we go back in there to get your stuff."

"My stuff?" I wipe my nose and look at him bewildered.

He grips my neck softly rubbing it with the pad of his

thumb. "You're staying with me until we know you'll be safe in your apartment."

I give him a hug. "Thanks, Dylan. I don't know what I'd do if . . ." I don't finish my sentence, just leave it implied. Dylan shakes his head like it's not necessary. I dial 911. After a while, the cops make it to my apartment and it's officially a crime scene. The police officers look quizzically at Birdie. I watch them step over broken glass and all my items strewn on the floor. I cry as they gather evidence. Dylan takes me into the hall and hugs me tight.

After giving our statements, we are free to go. I pack a small duffle bag of a few clean clothes that are still in my drawers. I take one last look at my ravaged apartment. I'm quiet most of the way back. Dylan carries Birdie and holds my hand all the way to his apartment.

We make it into his place and I just stand in the middle of his living room, not knowing what to do. Birdie is cozied up in her bed and Dylan just watches me with his hands in his pockets. That's when the waterworks start really flowing. I'm bawling my eyes out. Dylan looks concerned. He comes to me and wipes my tears away. He holds my face and I look into his eyes.

Dylan looks conflicted and unsure, but then he makes a decision. He slowly lowers his face to mine and gives me the sweetest kiss. I hold on to the back of his head and press him harder against me. I need to feel this and nothing else. I want to forget about my apartment and stop feeling this fear that has overtaken me within the last few hours.

He follows my cue and kisses me with vigor. I open my

mouth for him and slide my tongue across his lips. His hands dive into my hair and I'm lost in this kiss. Dylan slows the kiss and moves away from me. I grab his shirt and hold him in front of me.

"Andy, you've just been through a traumatic experience. I think we need to calm down and go to sleep for the night." He says the words, but I can see he wants this as bad as I do right now. I move and start to kiss down his neck. "Andy . . ." He's giving me a warning, but I ignore it. He finally steps back.

"Dylan, I need this. Please help me forget about it. I want you." I just want to be with him like this. I don't want to think about my apartment or the things that are gone. The items I'm going to have to replace. How much money this is going to cost me or if they will ever find the perpetrator. How did someone get in my apartment in the first place? I just need to forget all these questions and feel his body against mine. I need to feel safe and I do with him.

"Sweetie . . ." I hear him wavering and I dive in for the kill. Slowly I remove my red panties. He stares down at the piece of fabric on his floor. Grabbing his shirt, I walk backward until I hit the back of his door. My lips land on his and he starts to move. I'm hoisted up against his door. I wrap my legs around his waist. Dylan undoes his buckle and his pants, then he's thrusting into me.

I groan against his ear. Dylan's hands move to my ass as he grips so hard, I know there will be marks. It's wild and hot. He's pulling at the top of my dress until my breasts are exposed. He's sucking on them as he fucks me against his door. We're both grunting so loud, I'm sure we are keeping his neighbors awake. His door is taking a beating as is my body. It's exquisite.

"Fuck, Andy. Shit."

"Oh, Oh!" I squeeze my eyes shut as the orgasm wave hits me head on. My head falls back and hits against the door. His hand comes up to grab my neck to pull me away from it. Then, we're moving again. He lays me down on the kitchen table and rips my dress right down the middle. Dylan goes to town on my breasts as he continues pumping. He pulls his shirt off over his head and continues fucking me. He's like the Energizer Bunny.

My body starts to move across the table. Dylan grabs my legs to bring me back to the edge. This is what I need. I'm only able to think about our bodies moving against each other. I hear our pants and moans echo across his loft. I hold on to the table until my fingers are burning. He begins to rub my clit and I can feel the ascension of another orgasm. "Don't stop, Dylan. Oh. My. God," I cry out.

"All night, baby. All. Night." He thrusts with those last two words and I hit the peak. I'm thrashing all over the table and clawing at his arms, back, and shoulders.

"Yes." Dylan pulls away from my body and looks down at my pussy. His eyes close and his mouth drops open as he strokes his cock over my body. His other hand grips my hip like a vice. I don't care how hard he's squeezing me right now, because I'm staring at his amazing face in ecstasy. Cum shoots out and lands on my stomach.

9

"That's gotta be some kind of record or something," I say after our last round of sex.

"What's that?" he mumbles, his face buried in the comforter after we used the last condom in his drawer.

I turn to lay my chest on his back. God, he smells good even though we've been at it for hours. Even the smell of his sweat turns me on. What the hell is up with that? Boys are usually so stinky, but he's all man. "I said that has to be a record."

His face turns toward me, away from the blanket. "Yeah, we may have sprained my dick. Like seriously, I can't feel it. My balls ache something fierce. Shit." He turns over. As he does, I am rolled over. I'm stretched across his stomach with my butt in the air. "Mmmm. Now this is more like it." He smacks my butt twice and then rubs my cheeks. I turn and look at his cock and sure enough, he's hard again.

"Umm, yeah. I don't think it's sprained." Pushing off

him, I collapse on to my side of the bed. *My side of the bed? What am I thinking? I don't have a side.*

"I need food. Then we can talk about my dick some more and we can try that cowgirl position on my couch, because that shit was hot. I'd also like to try fucking you while we play video games. I think it will give me an advantage."

I pinch his nipple. "Ouch! What?" He grabs my hand.

I really don't know what we are doing anymore. Are we dating? Is this some fucked-up colleagues with benefits? What about my apartment? I take a deep breath and exhale.

"I hate to bring this up, but what are we doing?" I know I sound like such a girl right now . . . and you know what, maybe that's okay. We need to figure out what we are doing here. I don't know what the rules are, or if they are any. It's confusing. We had amazing sex last night and then he seemed to get pissed that I was leaving. Then he was an asshole again. But when I needed him most, Dylan was there and he helped me forget . . . a lot. Like I really lost count of how many orgasms I had after ten. It was crazy. We fucked against his door, the kitchen table, kitchen counter, the fridge. That one was pretty cold but it came in handy when he wanted whipped cream. We finally moved to his bedroom, the shower, then the bed. All over the bed actually. We ended up on the floor. The sheets pulled off and everything.

It was like we were trying to get inside each other's bodies. It was wild and primal and necessary. Our bodies had to have the other. I couldn't stop coming and he couldn't stop fucking and it was the best sex I've ever had. Now I'm sitting here wondering what this all means. I mean I'd love to continue like this, but I know it's not feasible. We do have to be in a work environment together and I need to do something about my apartment. I can't stay here.

"Ugh, does this have to have a label, Andy?" Dylan sighs and drapes his arm over his face to try and block me out.

I sit up a little annoyed, but not surprised by his reaction. "I don't have to have a label. I just need to know what the rules are or parameters."

"Surprisingly, when you talk like that it makes me hard again. Do you have reading glasses? I would love to fuck you as a librarian. You can talk about parameters while I pound you from behind. Here roll over."

He makes a grab at me, but I quickly jump up. Of course, I'm naked and all that does is make him stare at my breasts.

"Ugh! No."

"No, you don't have glasses? Well that's a shame. Here come jump on my stick anyway," he says while stroking himself.

I have my hands on my hips now. I'm trying not to be turned on by him touching himself in front of me. It's not really working. Dylan can turn me on with just a look.

"No, I mean no we need to talk about this."

"Ugh." Dylan sadly stops his ministrations and falls back on the bed. "Okay, fine. We have a good working relationship. I would like to keep that as is. After hours though we can fuck like bunnies. I'm looking forward to fucking you into a gaming handicap."

"I can't stay here though, Dylan. I need to go back to my place. I'm here too much. I'm sure I'll suffocate you." I sit down beside him on the bed.

"I liked it when you suffocated me last night with your pussy. That was fantastic." I slug him in the side. "Ouch. Okay, fine. We'll call the police department and see if they have any new information. We'll get you a new lock for your front door. I think we should also buy you some pepper spray just in case."

I'm stunned. He used the word "we" three times. I don't really want to point that out and scare him off, but this is sounding more and more like a boyfriend/girlfriend relationship. Would I want to be Dylan's girlfriend? That's just weird. I'll leave it at that, but that has to be one of the sweetest things any guy has said to me. On that note, I change tactics and decide to get my hands dirty.

"What are you . . . ? Oh, fuck. Yeah, sweetie just like that. Mmmm, you can't get enough of this cock, can you? I love your mouth."

With that, I show him how much I appreciate him.

～

We contact the police department and find out that there has been a string of burglaries in my area. More specifically, in my building. Dylan doesn't like that news. He convinces me to stay with him by using his tongue. He says I can wake up every morning to him "going downtown." Needless to say, I relent.

We got a new lock on my door anyway and cleaned up my apartment. Well, I cleaned up my apartment while Dylan counted all the pink items in my place. I grabbed some clothes and toiletries and semi moved in with Dylan. The whole scenario is so bizarre. Dylan used to hate being around me and now I'm living with him, not to mention working with him during the week as well.

It's been two weeks and everything is going smoothly. Weirdly enough, he's really fun to live with. I didn't realize how alone I felt until I moved in with him. There's always someone to lend a hand or get feedback on an outfit. It's quite nice. I've never lived with a guy. I thought it would be horrible.

I can't say that we have stuck to his rules about keeping our work relationship the same. Sometimes he will get off a heated call and stalk over to me. Bend me over my desk and fuck me until everything is off my desk and on the floor. He just calls it an occupational hazard.

This new Dylan is driving me wild. And he's been really sweet. I feel like he really cares about me and wants to make sure I'm taken care of. Birdie's in heaven. She loves Dylan and his loft. He's always giving her cuddles and a new toy. He doesn't think I notice, but her bed is full of toys I never purchased.

Whenever we fight over something it always ends in sex. In my past relationships, it was never like this. If I had an argument with someone, we would hash it out and come to a resolution or not and then be done with it, usually with me still being pissed. It's difficult to be mad at Dylan when he makes me speechless by lifting up my skirt and kissing my who-ha.

God, he's insatiable. He says I am, but he's ready to go all the time. I've never had this much sex in my life. Not even that one summer when I was going through some changes and my hormones were off the charts. I masturbated a crap load then.

Birdie rubs against my leg as I shut down my computer for the day. Dylan is already playing video games. Our numbers have been really good. It seems this transition has been a smooth one. It's still hard to believe I work for him. He's a good boss; fair and precise. He knows what he wants and he knows how to get it too. I really do admire the way he's on the phone with people.

We've looked into a couple of different locations for offices. I've even contacted Cindy to come work for us. I've kept in touch with her since our jobs terminated. She didn't seem surprised that Dylan and I work so well together. She's a dear friend and I'm really looking forward to working with her again when we decide on a new location.

"Sniper," I call out to him. A second later he gets shot in the head and his avatar dies.

Dylan turns his head and he has a smirk on his face. I smile back. "Why don't you show me how it's done, Andy?"

"Okay." I'm always up for gaming. I haven't in a while since we've been humping like rabbits. I kneel down next to him behind the coffee table. He hands over the controller. I immediately start picking up guns and going to my hideout location. This map is a sniper's playground. I'm not going to give them an advantage if I can help it. I subconsciously notice that Dylan has moved from his spot. I feel his hands at my waist. I look back at him since he's behind me.

"I'm your handicap, babe. It's not fair to the other players. I'm evening the field. Now lean over the coffee table and spread your legs." I hear my player die but do as Dylan says. My core is already aching for him. I'll play along, but I won't promise that I'll be invested in this game. When he touches me, everything else goes to the background. "That's my girl. Now I'm just going to push these sweet pink panties aside and . . ." He rubs his dick against my folds. I moan. He notices I'm already wet and pushes inside me. I gasp. "Play, princess," he mumbles as he nibbles around my ear. I pick up the controller from where I've dropped it on the table and start to shoot at some of the other players.

He thrusts into me quickly and I drop the controller again. He makes a *"tsk, tsk"* sound and I try and get my head back in the game. I'm not going to let him get to me. Then he starts to rub my clit. "Ohmygod." It feels amazing and it's taking everything in me to concentrate on this stupid game. I'm so glad I don't have a headset and mic on right now. The other players would definitely know what's going on.

Luckily, I find a rocket launcher and go to town on the other team. That's when Dylan starts thrusting with earnest. I'm breathing heavy. The controller vibrates in my hands and notice I'm being shot at. I pull the trigger and take the guy out. It's the last kill and the one to win it. I drop the controller and grind my hips back into him.

"Dylan." His hands are braced against the table on both sides of me. I'm caged in and loving his body over me. I twist my head to kiss him. Our tongues mingle and I'm getting more and more wet. He's going too slow for me and I'm getting antsy. I move away from him. His face is confused, until I push him down on the floor. I sit astride him and slide down his hard cock.

"Fuck, Andy. Yes, ride my dick." He pushes my shirt up and pulls my bra cups down. My breasts are exposed as he fondles them. I lean down over him so he can put one in his mouth. He complies and I start to feel the pull of my orgasm. "Mmmm, baby. I can feel you're about to come."

I go up in flames and make sounds I didn't even know I could as I ride him to pure ecstasy. He gets me every time he talks dirty to me. I love it. I'll have dreams about his dirty mouth and then wake him up to have sex. He smacks my ass and starts a punishing rhythm from below. I've collapsed on his chest, a heady mess. Dylan is the only man who I want inside me all the time. None of my other lovers can even compare to the type of sexual connection we have.

"Fuck, baby. I can feel your juices running down my balls. God, you're so fucking hot." He grunts a few times and clenches his eyes shut. I always try and watch him when he comes. It almost makes me come again. "Holy shit, holy shit. Fuck." I'm braced above him now, just watching his face and trying to move with him. He stills and his entire body quivers. "Holy fuck, Andy. I just double orgasmed. Can you believe that shit? Holy crap. I've never done that before. Shit. We need to do that again." I smile and collapse on top of him. I've heard stories of guys being able to come more than once, but I didn't think they were true. He rubs my back and kisses my hair. I still won that game. Two points for Team Pink!

10

*T*hings are really good between us. Who would've thought that Dylan and I would be a couple? Although, he's never stated we are. We don't go on dates and we haven't met each other's family or friends for that matter. Is he keeping me a secret? Are we even a couple? He's never called me his girlfriend.

"Are you my boyfriend, Dylan?" We are lying in bed. I've been living with him for a month and I still don't know what we're doing. Are we just fucking? It's driving me insane. I want to know if this is going somewhere. I don't want to get too comfortable with this situation. He hasn't given me any cues that this is a long-term thing.

"Do we have to put a label on this, Andy? I don't do girlfriends or anything. I don't know what you want me to say." He sounds tired and irritated. It still stings that he doesn't see this as anything more than casual. I want to be someone's girlfriend. I want a guy to take me out on a date and call it that. I don't want to be an easy lay or convenient. Maybe Dylan isn't man enough.

I get up out of his bed. I don't feel comfortable here anymore. This isn't my space. He isn't my boyfriend. We are nothing. I need to get back to my place and sort things out. I can't be around him right now. I'm too upset. Without a word, I get dressed.

"Andy, what are you doing?" He sits up in bed. Once I grab my bag and start stuffing things in it, I think it becomes pretty apparent. "Come on, Andy. It's ten o'clock at night. You can't leave right now. Why don't you lie back down and we'll go for round two?"

That infuriates me more. He does think of this as just sex. I mean nothing more to him than a quick lay, a warm body. "Fuck you. I deserve more than this." He looks taken aback. I don't think I've ever been this mad with anyone in my life. He's just throwing this all away.

He stands next to the bed with just some black boxers on. "Because I won't call you my girlfriend? Are you serious?" I don't answer him. I go to the bathroom to grab all my things. When I come out he's pacing beside the bed.

"I deserve to be someone's girlfriend." I push past him and grab Birdie, who's asleep in her bed. She snorts at me and wiggles, but I have a good hold so she can't run off. I know she wants to stay with Dylan, but I can't. He's made it clear what this situation is. I no longer want to be a part of it. I turn to look at him. Wait and see what he does. He stands there with his hands on his hips, angry.

He's not going to stop me. He's letting me go. I can feel my tears coming. I quickly leave and shut the door behind me. I make it downstairs and then I start to bawl. I've never felt this heartbroken. I feel unwanted. I thought he thought this was special. I thought he thought I was important. He doesn't care. All those things I saw in him, I was being delusional.

At my apartment it's quiet. My stomach feels a bit queasy after the last time I was alone like this. Thankfully, my door is locked. It's pitch black in my apartment. I turn on the entry light and place Birdie down. She hobbles over to her little bed by the TV and lies down with a huff. She's not happy to be back and honestly, I'm not either. But I'm not going to stay with someone just because we have great sex. There has to be more to it. Mutual respect and eventually love needs to happen for me to want to stay with a guy. Dylan was giving me none of that.

I pour myself a glass of wine, sit down on the couch and turn the TV on for background noise. My phone goes off in my purse and I reluctantly get up and get it. It's Dylan. I hit ignore. He calls again and I send him to voicemail again. Next, I get an alert to a text.

Dylan: I just want to make sure you made it home ok.

I wail. I fall to the couch and bawl my eyes out. Birdie even comes over to me to make sure I'm okay. I grab a tissue from a box beside the couch and wipe my face. He has to go and do something sweet like make sure I made it home okay. Of course, I wouldn't even be here if he would just man up and admit we had a relationship. I text him.

Andy: I'm home.

Dylan: Ok, let me know if you need anything.

I don't know what to reply, so I don't. It's a Tuesday night and I have work in the morning. I decide that I will go in as per usual. I can't afford not to have a job right now. If he's going to act like we're nothing, then I can do it too. We will stay strictly professional from now on.

∽

I knock on his door at eight a.m. on the dot. After a minute, I pound on the door. There's some shuffling and he opens his door in his boxers. His hair is a mess and he smells like alcohol. "Andy. You're back." I wave my hand in between us to clear the air. The alcohol smell is overpowering. He opens the door and let's Birdie and me in.

I'm three steps in and he grabs me from behind and starts kissing me on the neck. Normally, I wouldn't be able to resist those kisses, but since he smells like alcohol and I'm pissed as hell, I turn from his grasp. I slap him across the face. I don't know what's gotten into me, but that's the reaction I give him. I've never slapped anyone before.

He stands there with his hand against his cheek and a dumbfounded expression on his face. "Ow. What the hell, Andy?"

"I will not be manhandled at work. This is strictly

professional. I'm not your girlfriend." I turn and walk to my desk and set my things down to start up my computer. Dylan leaves to go to his room. It's a typical day. I check e-mails, file some paperwork and work on a few contracts. An hour later Dylan comes out. He's freshly showered and dressed for a day at work.

It starts as a normal work day. We ignore each other for the most part and get down to business. As lunchtime comes around it gets a little shaky. Most of the time we would have sex during lunch and then he or I would go grab lunch to go and bring it back. Today is a different story though. I can feel his eyes on me. I purposely bend over my desk to get a file. I hear him sigh.

Okay, so I might be teasing him a little, but he deserves it. "Andy? How long are you going to keep this no sex thing going?" I huff at him and ignore what he just said. I feel his body behind me. "Are you going to slap me again if I touch you?"

"Maybe." I try and hide my smile but can't. I still can't believe I slapped him. I feel bad now.

"I missed you being in my bed last night." Turning around, I look at him and cross my arms.

"I bet you did."

His hands are in his pockets. Dylan looks vulnerable. "I'm being serious here, Andy. I missed you. Not the sex or your body, even though that's part of it. Look, I'm not doing very good here." He takes a deep breath. "I want you to be my girlfriend." He exhales loudly.

Was that seriously that hard for him to do? What

happened to him in previous relationships where he's afraid of having a girlfriend?

"Dylan, I don't want to be your *girlfriend* just so you can fuck me. I want to go on dates and tell each other things and you introduce me as someone special in your life. Not just your assistant."

He steps closer to me. "You don't think I know that? I've never had a girlfriend, Andy. Never. I don't know how to do this shit. I've never wanted to call anyone my girlfriend until you left last night. I realized what a simple request that really was and I was being an ass. I was still somewhat out of it from my bender last night and that's why I acted like that this morning. That slap woke me up. I just thought I'd let you cool off for a bit and then broach the subject later. I'm not good at this . . . relationships."

I smile at him. "I think you're doing fine."

He smirks.

He steps toward me as he talks. "I want to take you on dates and introduce you as my girlfriend. I want to tell you things." He's hovering above my lips. "Can I kiss you? I want to touch you so bad."

I love sweet Dylan. I'm melting in my panties. "Yes," I exhale. He pushes me and my back hits my desk. "Dylan? What are you doing?"

"I didn't say where I wanted to kiss you." His eyes gleam as he moves my dress up my legs. "Holy shit. You're not wearing panties. You dirty girl. You drive me crazy." He kisses the top of my legs. I purposely didn't wear panties today because I knew sooner or later he'd find out and it would drive him insane. Call it payback by underwear.

"Dylan." I run my hand through his hair.

"Shhh, I'm going down on my girlfriend." I moan at that last word and start grinding my hips against his face. "Mmmm, you missed me, baby?"

"Yes." I love make up sex. It's the best. It strikes me as odd that Dylan hasn't ever had a girlfriend. I'll have to ask him about that later, when my legs aren't around his head.

His lips surround my pussy and he lightly sucks. Dylan moves in circular motions around my clit and I'm gone. I chant his name over and over again until my climax subsides. He moves up my body and kisses me. I taste my release and it gets me even more wanton. I unbuckle his belt and pull his cock out. I rub him against my wet center as he rocks back and forth, creating friction. He spins me around so I'm leaning over the desk and starts pounding me from behind. I love desk sex. It makes me feel so naughty. We both come together with papers and files flying everywhere.

"I love fucking my girlfriend's pussy," he says on a sigh. I return his sigh and start cleaning up my desk as we get back to work. Dylan is my boyfriend. I smile at the thought. I have a sexy, sweet boyfriend. I'm blissfully happy in this moment.

I don't know what's gotten into me lately. I'm up and down and so horny. Dylan is just driving me crazy. I'm glad we are official though and are clear with what we want in this relationship. I think I knew last night that I was starting to fall in love with him. It scared me. He's nowhere near close to feeling that for me. I freaked out and left, but I can't stay away. He's like a ninja that creeped into my heart. I can see us growing old together and maybe married. Honestly, I don't even know if he's the marrying type. It was hard enough for him to admit we were even in a relationship.

He seems the type of guy that would be completely content with just living with a girl and not needing to make it official. Dylan is probably one of those guys that thinks that a piece of paper means nothing. Of course, I don't think I could ever broach that subject with him. He would probably black out from his commitment phobia.

I think if I was with the right person, I wouldn't need that piece of paper either. I could live happily with Dylan, with or without a piece paper. We aren't even close to being there yet. I like what we have now and I think he's happy too.

Dylan's leaning over the dining room table and checking out a few listings available for office space. I smile and feel that little flutter feeling again. *Yup, he's gotten to me.*

11

It's two weeks later and since my period was a no show, I'm now holding a pregnancy test. We've been very careful. After that first week, we had to keep buying boxes of condoms so I decided to get on birth control pills and he got tested. Then we were doing it like bunnies all over his apartment. I had never gone bare before with a guy. It was Earth shattering. He hadn't gone bare before either. We pretty much stayed in bed all that afternoon, feeling every inch of each other, inside and out.

But now I'm looking at two little lines that seem to say I'm pregnant. I heave into the toilet like I did yesterday morning. This is the worst thing that could happen right now. Dylan just agreed to be in a relationship and now I'm pregnant. He's going to think I trapped him or something and I'm not ready for a baby right now. I've always dreamed about being a mother, but when I'm married and the relationship is clearly defined and I'm financially stable. Thankfully, I have paid off all my school loans and still have my apartment. Dylan pays me very well. I'm more secure financially than I ever have been. I'm still not ready to be a mother, but I don't think I could ever consider terminating the pregnancy or giving this baby up for adoption. I should probably make a doctor's appointment just to make sure; I don't want to freak him out on false information. I think these tests can be wrong sometimes.

I make an appointment for the next available slot which happens to be at the end of the week. So I have to wait a whole three days before I can get confirmation. It's going to be a long week. How am I going to stay calm and not tell Dylan until then? I wrap up the pregnancy test in some tissue and put it in my panty drawer. I took the test while Dylan went to go get us some lunch and he should be back any minute. Now, if I can just act semi normal around him.

It took about thirty minutes for him to notice anything. "Why are you acting so weird?" Dylan is giving me a pinched face look. I gaze down at my food and move it around my takeout box.

"I'm not acting weird. I'm just not that hungry." He gives me the stink eye like he knows something's up. I'm totally fucked right now. Then that gives me an idea.

"God, you've been so horny lately. It's awesome." Dylan pushes into me again as I lie across the dining table, our takeout boxes long forgotten and shaking against Dylan's punishing rhythm. "Fuck, Andy. You make me so hot. If I knew calling you my girlfriend would up the sex, I would have done it earlier. Shit. I'm gonna come."

I moan as my orgasm rips through me. He pulses inside me and I'm reminded of what else I might be keeping inside me. I start to weep.

I cry a lot, really at the drop of a hat. I'm just a sensitive person. I'm hoping this won't alert him that anything is wrong or that I'm upset about anything. Calming myself down, I play it off as just an amazing orgasm.

"What's wrong, baby? Why are you crying? Did I hurt you?" He leans over me and wipes at my tears. I can't keep this from him any longer. I'm breaking down right here before his eyes. I'm a terrible liar. I can't keep a secret to save my life either. I don't know why I thought I could do this. Maybe it won't be that bad? It would be nice to share this information with someone else. I've only had the burden for a couple of hours and I'm already overwhelmed. I should just tell him what's going on so we can deal with this together.

Of course I do what I shouldn't do and just blurt it out. "I'm pregnant!"

He immediately pales and looks down where we are currently connected. He pulls out and nearly falls over twice as he puts his boxers and pants on. His hands slam on his hips once he rights himself. Oh no. This doesn't look good. I rise and pull down my dress so I'm covered.

"Want to run that by me again?" He looks pissed. His face is a little red and sweaty. I'm not sure if it's from the sex or what I just told him. I slink off the table and grab my takeout box for something to do. "What are you doing?" he asks me incredulously.

"I'm just putting this in the fridge for later." I don't know what the hell I'm doing. For some reason my mind wants to act like I didn't say anything and for everything to go back to normal, but Dylan is not having any of it.

"What the fuck, Andy? You just told me you're pregnant and your acting like nothing has changed." He's pacing in front of the dining table now. Birdie rouses from her bed by my desk and goes over to try and comfort Dylan. She can tell he's upset. She rubs up against his leg. "Not now, Birdie." He shoves her with his leg. I gasp and call Birdie over to me.

"Look, I didn't plan for any of this to happen, but you don't need to take it out on Birdie. She was just trying to calm you down."

"Calm down?"

I stand up with Birdie while Dylan looks like he's about to pull his hair out.

"Did you just seriously say I need to calm down?"

"No . . . I—" Dylan cuts me off mid-sentence.

"You just told me you're pregnant for God's sake, while I was still inside you."

"I don't see . . ."

"Who the fuck does that? Don't answer that." He turns his back on me. I'm standing there dumbfounded. I knew he might freak out a little bit and it might take some adjusting and definitely some planning. I just didn't think he would lash out. "Did you stop taking your birth control?"

I narrow my eyes at him as he turns back around. "No."

"Well, how the fuck, Andy?"

"I don't know. I take my birth control pills every day. I just took the test this morning. It could be false. I have a doctor's appointment on Friday to confirm." I'm making excuses and telling him all my plans so he knows I didn't try and trap him, but I don't think any of what I've said is any comfort to him at all. I can tell by his face he doesn't want this baby. I'm going to be raising this child on my own. There's a shift in the room. I don't know if it's my attitude toward this situation or his, but I know we're done here.

I turn to go in our bedroom . . . or his bedroom. I pack a bag of all my clothes. I still hadn't fully moved in with him. It doesn't take me long to grab everything I need. He's giving me space which is good. I'm trying to keep it together and not cry. I take one last look at the bed we have shared for the past month. My eyes start to water and I look up to the ceiling to gain control. When I walk out of the bedroom, Dylan spots the bag I'm carrying.

"Where are you going?" Dylan's still by the dining table with his hands on his waist. He hasn't moved at all since we started this argument, discussion, breakup, whatever this is.

"Home. Come on, Birdie." Birdie comes to me immediately, probably sensing the hurt in my voice. I clip her pink leash on her. Dylan just stands there. I'm a little surprised at his lack of emotion on me leaving. That solidifies that he doesn't want a baby or me.

"Let me know how the doctor's appointment goes." My mouth gapes open with my back turned to him and the tears start to fall. I feel like I'm being taken out with the trash. I've never felt so low in my life. He must feel nothing for me at all for him to not even suggest coming with me or seeing me before my appointment. I guess it was just sex for him. If he wants to know about my appointment, he can come and figure it out for himself. I will not seek out some deadbeat asshole. I close the door behind me.

12

My appointment on Friday came and went. The doctor did confirm that I am pregnant. She gave me a lot of pamphlets and prenatal vitamins. She cheered me up a little with all the appointments I have to look forward to. I can't wait to have a sonogram; I'm wondering if it's going to be a girl or a boy. I haven't told anyone about the baby. I haven't spoken to my dad since Christmas and I don't see him being thrilled about being a grandfather. I don't even think he liked being called father.

I can't help but smile knowing that I'm going to be a mother. I was scared and shocked at first about this baby, but I'm looking forward to witnessing another being's firsts. The first time the baby says "Mama," crawls, tries solid food, walks. After the doctor's appointment, I was happier about this than when I was going into the appointment. I've officially got baby fever.

I haven't heard anything from Dylan since I left that

Tuesday afternoon. I've cried every night and vomited almost every morning, but during the day I find my strength and get on with what needs to be accomplished. I've been looking for a job. I have insurance still, but I don't want to depend on *his* insurance much longer. I need to cut ties with him completely. He pretty much stomped on my heart and threw it in the dumpster. I'm keeping it together solely for the baby growing inside me.

I decide to call Cindy. She's had a couple of children; she might be able to give me some advice. I could really use a friend right now. "Hey, Cindy."

"Hi, Andy. How's the windy city treating you and Birdie? Is Dylan hiring for his new office yet?"

I know Cindy has been looking forward to Dylan's firm expanding and I have mentioned that he was looking for some help. I don't really know what to tell her, except the truth.

"Well, I'm not really working with Dylan anymore. We had a bit of a falling out and I'm on the hunt now too."

"That's a shame. What happened? I thought things were going really well. Is he being an asshole again?" She laughs. I used to complain to her all the time how horrible he was and it seems things never change.

"You could say that. I'm pregnant and he was upset. I left and haven't heard from him since." I sniffle. God, I sound so pathetic. It sounds like a shitty soap opera. I grab a tissue next to me as Birdie sidles up to my lap. I'm sitting down in my living room checking on my laptop for any open positions.

"I'm sorry, sweetie. It's tough being a single mom. I

should know. Don't you worry, you're not alone. I can't believe he would just let you go like that." Cindy knew we were involved. Since she's my only friend here in Chicago, I kept her up to date including when we became boyfriend and girlfriend. That seems so long ago now.

"Assholes never change, Cindy. I thought he was different too, but I was wrong. I'm due in June." I sigh. What am I going to do?

"Oh, a June baby. That will be wonderful. Don't you worry. Stress is not good for the baby. Just let me know if there's anything I can do to help. You know, I've had my share of babies." She laughs. "If I see any positions that I think you'd be good for, I'll let you know."

"Thanks, Cindy. That goes for me too. If I see jobs for you, I'll call you first thing. I really appreciate your support. I don't really have anyone here, except you. Thanks for being a good friend."

"Oh, don't even mention it, honey. I know how hard it is out there. Us women need to stick together. Keep me updated on the baby, okay?"

I agree and promise to call her next week after my next appointment. I smile after I hang up. At least I have one friend I can count on. Now, back to looking at the want ads.

Sometimes, late at night I wonder if he even thinks about us or if he's already moved on and has a girl in his bed every night like he seemed to have before. He probably has already fucked a few other girls by now.

I didn't give him any notice I was no longer going to be coming into work either. I'm sure he figured it out when he didn't hear back from me on Friday. It's been over a week since I said goodbye and although I've eaten all the ice cream in my freezer, things aren't as bad as they seemed at first. I can't seem to watch any romantic movies or *Die Hard* since they remind me of Dylan. Instead I'm watching Disney movies. I look forward to showing my child *Cinderella* and *Snow White*. I guess they're somewhat romance movies, but the struggle these princesses went through to make it out on the other side, I can relate to.

I'm in the middle of *Cinderella*. She's dancing with the prince and singing about love. I'm eating popcorn and snuggled next to Birdie, when there's a knock on the door. I look at Birdie and she looks at me. She goes to the door and wags her little pink tail.

"Who is it, girl?" I know she must smell whoever is on the other side of the door. Looking through the peephole, I'm surprised to see Dylan on the other side gripping both sides of my doorframe. He's a bit disheveled. He also looks mad. I'm not sure I want to open the door. "What do you want, Dylan?" I keep the door closed and watch his reaction to my question.

"Come on, Andy. Let me in, please." He bows his head and I can no longer see his face. I still don't want to let him in. Why is he here now?

"What do you want, Dylan?" I sound tired and frustrated. I don't want to be dealing with this right now, I have an interview tomorrow for a great position at a top accounting firm.

"How was the doctor's appointment?" He looks straight through the peephole at me.

I shiver and collect myself. "Fine, good. I'm still pregnant." I guess he wanted to make sure I was still pregnant. Maybe he's having difficulty with the business and wanted me to come back and work if I wasn't pregnant. Guys are such assholes.

"Can I come in and talk to you, please?" He stands up straight and puts his hands in his pockets.

"We don't have anything to talk about, Dylan. I'm keeping the baby and you don't have to worry about any responsibility with this child. I'm willing to do it on my own." I lean my forehead against the door and wait for him to leave.

"Baby, let me in."

I don't know if it's hormones or just plain anger, but when he calls me baby, something happens and I can't control my actions. I swing open the door and charge at him. His eyes go wide and I slap him in the face. His hand goes to his cheek and his eyes close.

"Okay, I deserve that. I know I've been an asshole, but I . . ."

"No!" I point my finger in his face and he flinches slightly. I back off a bit, slightly embarrassed of my behavior. I don't normally lash out like this. I'm a civil person and he just brings out the crazy in me, I guess. Taking a few deep breaths, I grit my teeth. "Do not call me baby. I'm not your baby. We broke up. This, whatever it was between us, fuck buddies, it's over. And while you're at it, you can find yourself another secretary." I turn and slam the door behind me and wait until I hear his footsteps retreating. I sigh and slide down the door and bawl my eyes out. That bastard just had to come here and make me cry.

The next day, I get through my interview surprisingly well. The staff seems very happy and the company has great benefits. I get a call later that evening with a job offer and I readily accept. Then that evening there's another knock on my door. Slowly, I approach my door afraid it's Dylan again. I hear his voice before I look out the peephole.

"Andy, I thought I'd let you cool off before we spoke anymore. I don't want you to be stressed right now."

"I'm cool as an Eskimo," I reply. *Eskimo? Where the hell did that come from?* He's not ruining my day. I just got a new job and I'm on the road to a secure future for me and my baby. I called Cindy earlier to tell her the good news and she was also happy to relay to me that she had also found a new position. Things were looking up for us both.

"Can I please come in?" I stand and think about this for a moment. Hopefully, he's just saying goodbye and wants to leave with a clear conscience. The sooner I got this over with the better. I really don't want him banging on my door anymore. I'm so over his asshole tendencies. I slowly unlock my door and open it wide for him. "Thank you." Dylan gives me a small smile.

I follow him into the living room where he plops down in the middle of the couch. I sit in the chair adjacent to him. We sit there for a moment, just looking at each other. Dylan finally breaks the silence.

"How are you feeling?" I'm guessing he's really asking about the baby and not me.

"The baby is fine. I go in for another appointment next week. Don't worry, I've already found another job with good benefits. We'll be fine." Surprisingly, I sound confident. I don't feel that way at all. I hope he can't see through my facade.

"I asked how you're feeling, Andy." I ignore his question and stand up to let him know I'm done talking. There's nothing else to say. It's hard to look at him and still be angry with him. I keep repeating to myself that he's an ass and it helps. "Wait, Andy. Stop trying to run away from me. We need to talk about this like adults."

I turn slowly around from my path to the door. "What did you say?" Dylan rubs his face with his hands. He seems frustrated, but I don't care. I'm furious. I wouldn't be surprised if there was smoke coming out of my ears. "Did you just say that I need to talk like an adult?" I start to yell. "I'm not the one running away! I've been facing this since day one. You didn't want me or this baby. I left when I wasn't wanted. You're an irresponsible asshole! Get out!"

He rushes up from the couch to me. "You haven't even let me talk. I want to talk about this. I want to be involved with this baby too. I want to go to the appointments with you."

"What?" I stumble back away from him. He can't

mean that. He didn't want anything to do with us. Now Dylan wants to go to the appointments?

"I want to be involved in this baby's life. I'm the father. I didn't have one growing up and I won't do that to a child." I can't believe this. This should be good news, but I'm just being selfish. It'll be hard for my heart to be around him. I know it's what's best for the baby, it's just not good for me. That's what being a parent is. You make sacrifices for your child so that they can be happy, whatever's best for the baby.

"Fine. I'll text you when the next appointment is." I go to the door and open it for him. Dylan waits for a moment and then decides to walk out. He doesn't even look back. I guess that's all he came for. Well, at least he's decided to be a father to our baby. God, am I going to have to deal with him for the rest of my life? Will this pain ever ebb? I collapse on the sofa. Birdie accompanies me and I pet her. Before I know it, I've fallen asleep. I dream about a sweet little girl with my eyes and Dylan's dark hair. I dream of him with another woman visiting us. I'm alone with the baby and he's found another girlfriend. Waking up from that nightmare, I find it's dark outside my windows. The clock says it's eleven. Time to hit the hay.

Taking a quick shower, I tuck myself in bed. The entire night, I toss and turn and dream about me being eternally alone and Dylan having a new girl on his arm every time he comes to pick up our baby. The only thing I can think about is if that nightmare came true or worse, if he found one girl he wanted to be with. Tears fall on my pillow that night and every evening until my appointment the next week.

My new job doesn't start until the following week. I have a bit of time off to enjoy for a little while longer. This pregnancy so far has been tough. I still get sick every morning and I'm extremely tired throughout the day. I don't know how Cindy did it. I called her last night and she thought it was wonderful that Dylan was stepping up and is going to be involved. She could tell I was upset about the situation. She understood how I felt too. Cindy gave me some good advice to stay calm and healthy for the baby. Everything would work itself out.

So here I am outside of the OBGYN. There's no sign of Dylan and it's five minutes past our appointment. With a huff, I go inside and sign in. I'm brought back immediately and am instructed to undress from the waist down. I'm going to have a sonogram and since it's so early in my pregnancy they have to do it vaginally. Dylan still hasn't showed once the doctor walks in. I brush the tears from my eyes and put on a good face. If he's just going to flake out on us, he should've just left us alone.

There's a knock on the door before the doctor can walk me through the proceedings of our appointment. I cover my legs and pelvis with a pitiful scrap of paper, while a nurse pokes her head in the door.

"I'm sorry to bother you, doctor, but there's a man here that says he's the patient's boyfriend." I gasp. The doctor looks back at me and I nod. Why the hell would he say we're boyfriend and girlfriend? Then, he walks in. He takes my breath away. His beard is trimmed and he looks a little more rested than the last time he was at my door. Dylan looks a little out of breath.

"Hi. Sorry I'm late. I got stuck in traffic. It was hard finding a parking spot too." He kisses me on the forehead and sits down in the chair next to me. I give him a bewildered look. He's watching the doctor.

"Well, we were just about to start. You haven't missed anything." She turns to a machine with knobs and a screen on it. I quickly look back at Dylan.

He whispers, "I'm sorry. I didn't know if they'd let me back if I didn't say I was your boyfriend. There's was an accident downtown and I had to go the long way around." His eyes are pleading with me. I turn away and nod my head. At least he's here now, I guess. He grabs my hand and I pull away. Dylan mouths "Please." When I don't say anything, he leans into me. "I just want to hold your hand, Andy. Let me do that, please." His hand envelops mine once more and I let him. This is his way of being here for the baby. A tear runs down my cheek. I didn't even realize I was crying. I sniffle and wipe it away.

The appointment goes on without any surprises. I'm right on schedule and the baby is growing as expected. Dylan is quiet. Then we see our little peanut and a beating heart. I cry for the tenth time and Dylan seems awestruck. He grips my hand so tight I lose blood flow and have to hit his arm to release me. I'm so in love with this sweet little peanut already.

When the doctor is finished with my consult she steps out of the room. Sliding off the examination table, I hold on to the small sheet covering my modesty. I wait to see what Dylan is going to do. He stands still, waiting for me to get dressed. I clear my throat and I think he gets the hint.

"I'll meet you in the waiting room." He abruptly leaves. I sit down with my bare butt hanging out and bawl my eyes out. After a while, I finally pull myself together and quickly get dressed. I'm not looking forward to seeing Dylan out in the waiting room. It was tough enough having him here during this whole embarrassing ordeal. *Is it too much to ask to have my dignity intact?* On the other hand, I'm glad he was able to come. Even though, it would be easier on me if we went our separate ways, it's better for the baby to have a father.

I wish my father were more present in my life. Speaking of which, I haven't told him yet. He's going to be extremely disappointed in me. He of all people put work before family. My dad has no paternal instincts. I don't expect him to understand me being happy about having a baby even though I'm young. I know he wanted me to be set in a career but I was never as focused on that aspect of my life. I just wanted to live and enjoy my work, be able to pay the bills and maybe meet a nice boy someday. Obviously, that didn't happen.

I look at the picture the doctor gave me of our baby. I think I may have seen Dylan tear up too but he turned his head so I could no longer see his face. I hope he doesn't bail on me now. I really want him to commit to this. If he couldn't commit to me, I hope he's able to be a father to our child. He would be a really good dad if he tried. I sigh and walk out the door.

Dylan is leaning against the opposite side of the hallway. His eyes look grave. "Were you crying in there?" I try to control my reaction to him hearing me cry.

"I cry at the drop of a hat these days." I turn to walk to the nurse's desk to pay my copay. He follows. I don't think he bought that explanation.

I'm proved right when he asks, "Why were you crying, Andy?" I huff. I don't want to talk about this right now, let alone in the doctor's office. I tell him as much and he placates me by nodding his head. He tries to pay for my appointment, but I don't let him. It's silly, but I want to show him I can take care of myself. I thank the nurse after paying and we walk out the door.

"Why were you crying?" He turns to me.

"What do you want me to say, Dylan?" I cross my arms over my chest, feeling defensive. Does he expect me to rip my heart out for him? Put it on the chopping block for him to hammer to death? *Why couldn't you fight for me, for us? Why did you just let me go? Will you always be my constant reminder of my first love lost?* Wait. No. Ugh! I hate him. I love him. He's an ass. I walk toward the subway ignoring his lingering look.

"Andy, please. I know you're hurting and it's my fault. I'm sorry. I'd like you to come back and work for me."

"Are you crazy? Why would I work for you?" My finger jams in his face. I'm barely holding on to my wrath. I don't know how this man can get me so worked up. I'm usually very calm and collected but he drives me within an inch of insanity.

"It's not what it sounded like. I want to help you. I

want to see you. What if you went into labor and I wasn't there? I want to be able to make sure you're getting everything you need." My anger cools down a few notches. That was actually kind of sweet. I smile. Damn, these freaking mood swings. I'm up and down, hot and cold. I just need to get away from him to think. I can't think straight right now. I need ice cream. "You need ice cream?" Oh, shit. I must have said that out loud. I clench my eyes shut and take a deep breath.

"I appreciate your job offer, but I already have a good job and I don't think it would be a good idea to work together anymore. You know when the next doctor's appointment is. I guess I'll see you then?" I open my eyes and stare at his beard. God, I miss that beard between my legs. He nods a yes. "I'm going to get ice cream."

13

Two weeks later, I haven't had any more unexpected visits from Dylan. I'm a bit conflicted about that. It was nice when he was trying to see me, but it also hurt me every time I looked into his brown eyes. I dream about him almost every night, his body blanketing mine, keeping me safe. I miss his smell. Dylan smells like cinnamon. It's a strong yet comforting spice that makes me think of home, just like him. I huff and sit up in bed. I stretch my arms above my head and yawn.

Surprisingly, I've been sleeping really well. Maybe the dreams about Dylan help a little. I look over at my clock. It's seven forty-five. I need to get out of my cozy bed and get ready for work. I'm enjoying my new job at Hankman and Associates. They have incredible benefits. They have lunch catered almost every day. A girl can used to that.

They're trying to emulate Google in that aspect, make it a fun environment. None of us have cubicles; it's one long table we share with all our computers set in the middle. I'm not holed up in an office anymore. The people I work with are great too. They're all very friendly. I actually look forward to going to my job. I did with Dylan too, but I just couldn't work for him again. I wouldn't be able to face him day after day. I'd be fawning over him and he would be pushing me away.

Grudgingly, I roll out of bed and that's when I notice the blood. Everything goes black for a moment. I feel my body hit the cold floor. I break out in a sweat and start to shake. When I'm finally able to see my surroundings, I reach for my cell on the table near my bed. Sitting on the floor, I dial the one number I hate but need.

"Hello?"

"Dylan? Can you come over please?" Tears run down my face. I wipe my nose with the back of my hand and sniffle.

"Andy? Are you okay? I'm on my way." He wanted to stay on the line with me, but I told him I'd like to get changed before he arrived. I also need to call my doctor immediately and make an appointment. He reluctantly hangs up. As I'm pulling my shirt over my head, there's a knock rattling my door. "Andy?"

I sigh in relief and open the door wide. Dylan engulfs me in a huge hug, then pulls away slightly and cradles my face in his hands. "Are you okay? Did you speak with the doctor?" I nod and he moves his hands from my face to my sides. I feel a little guilty I'm keeping him in suspense a little longer so I can feel all this comfort from him.

"I have an appointment in thirty minutes. She was able to get me in quickly. She said spotting is normal with pregnancy, but she wants to check me over just to make sure." I lean my head on his shoulder. This is nice. I'm a lot calmer after talking to my doctor and with him here, I feel safe, reveling in his scent and warmth for a moment.

"Was it a lot of blood? Are you feeling okay?" Dylan's still amped up. I need to settle his nerves.

"I feel fine. It wasn't much blood." His arm wraps around my shoulders and he leads me out of my apartment.

"All right, let's get you to the doctor."

We get into his car and an hour later we're walking out of the exam room with smiles on our faces. It was just light spotting and nothing to worry about. The baby looked perfect. Dr. Flemming put our minds at ease. Dylan held my hand the entire time. It almost felt like we were a couple again. I tried to keep myself grounded. It wasn't too hard since my heart is still aching. I can't help but love him. My heart had no choice. It beats for him and this baby. It doesn't help how attentive he was this morning.

I honestly don't know what he wants from me anymore. Is he here only for the baby? Does he want a working relationship again? Does he want to be a couple again? I don't even know if that's on the table for me. This is all a big mess. Time away from him didn't help me come to a decision on any of this.

"Do you want to grab a late breakfast?" Dylan asks me as we are walking to his car. He opens the door for me and I slide in. I contemplate his question as he rounds the car. If time away from him didn't help, maybe time with him will help me figure out what I want out of all of this. When he buckles in his seat belt I answer him.

"Yes. That sounds nice." He smiles brilliantly at me and starts the car. That smile could melt panties off women everywhere.

We arrive at IHOP and are seated immediately. "I'm surprised you agreed to eat with me." Dylan puts cream and sugar in his coffee. I grab my hot chocolate and take a sip.

"I was hungry and you were willing to pay," I tease, taking a sip of my orange juice. No coffee for me these days. It's a small price to pay to have a healthy, happy baby. Dylan sits there and watches me for a moment. I don't know what he's up to, but he's smirking.

"You look beautiful, Andy." I look down at my flowy floral top that's the exact opposite of his black concert band T-shirt. I don't know what to make of that comment. I feel bloated and uncomfortable.

"Thank you." He takes a drink from his coffee and then plays with the cup by turning it on the table. He's stalling or trying to gather his words, I guess. He gives up on messing with his mug and steeples his hands in front of his mouth. It reminds me of Sherlock Holmes and I sigh. He's so hot, even when he's flustered and out of his element. He gives me a bewildered look and then shakes it off.

"You must know, I miss you like hell. It's been unbearable without you. I don't miss you as a secretary or a warm body in my bed or an easy lay as you put it awhile back. I miss my Andy. The smell of your skin in the morning and when you walk around in only my shirt. I even miss your pink shit everywhere. You shocked me with the way you told me you were pregnant."

I open my mouth to say something but he holds up his hand.

"Please, just let me finish." I nod and he continues. "I didn't react well. Honestly, I'm still in shock about it, but I want this. I want you and the baby. I want you to move in with me and let me take care of you. I'm a fucking idiot, I need a little bit of a learning curve on all this shit, Andy." He reaches out for my hand and I instinctively let him have it. He raises my hand to his mouth and kisses it. I've just turned to mush. This bearded tattooed Prince of Darkness is asking for pink in his house . . . and me. I begin to cry.

Dylan immediately abandons his seat across from me in the booth and joins my side to comfort me. I nestle into his neck and smell him in. He still smells like cinnamon and something else . . . something entirely him. "I love you." *Oh shit.* I just laid that on him. What the hell is wrong with me? Pregnancy. I'm blaming it on pregnancy hormones.

"What?" Dylan pulls away from me and looks me straight in the eye, waiting for confirmation of what I just blurted out.

"Umm, nothing. I've been craving pancakes all morning. I love pancakes." I peek up at him to see if he buys the lie. He scratches his jaw and looks down at me, bewildered.

"Huh. Well, the pancakes will be here shortly." He

laughs. I blow out some air and rest my head on his shoulder. Thank God he bought that. I don't know what I'd do if we addressed my love for him. He'd probably bolt on me. I hate to admit it, but I really do love him on my side with this baby. I need some support in this. It was a surprise to me too and it feels good to have someone like Dylan to share this with.

14

Dylan grabbed all my stuff from my apartment right after we left the pancake house and moved me and Birdie in immediately. She was happy as punch to be back at his loft, taking a place in his lap. He makes things easier for me and I do love him, whether he wants me to or not. I can't help it. I fell for the Neanderthal. I'm just hoping with time he'll love me too. Honestly, I think he already does. He just hasn't admitted it to himself yet. He builds up walls and that's why it's so difficult for him to express things, but I'm going to make it my mission to get this man to open up to me.

Right now, I have a different problem. It's been a week since I moved back in and we haven't had sex. What's up with that? He hasn't even hinted he wants anything physical. We cuddle on the couch and sleep in his bed every night, but he never makes a move. I've tried to get him worked up but he usually just turns me around and wraps his arms around me while he cradles my belly. It melts my heart and I don't want to move when he does that. It doesn't help that I'm crazy horny. It's no joke. I'm really suffering here. Something has to give.

"God, I love this movie." Dabbing my eyes with a tissue, I watch the train scene in *Mrs. Winterbourne*. Birdie is asleep in the other room, probably on Dylan's side of the bed. This feels like home. This man will sit next to me on the couch and watch a bona fide chick flick with me, but he won't admit yet that he loves me. I can live with that for now, as long as he keeps showing me every day. The words will come. Just thinking about him watching this with me makes me horny. His sweetness makes me horny. I rub his leg as he looks down at his phone. He's been begging me to come back and work for him, but I need my independence. I need to know that I can take care of this baby myself. I don't want to completely depend on a man to take care of me.

I begin to rub higher on his leg. He hasn't noticed yet and I want it that way. I want him horny just like I am, a slow and steady climb until he bursts with want for me and then it'll be on like Donkey Kong. I creep up his leg until I brush his manhood and I sigh. *Hello, old friend. I've missed you so much.* Dylan is still looking at his phone. I don't think he notices that his hips are moving slightly against my hand. I knew it! He's freaking horny too.

Before I know it, I've mounted Dylan and am rubbing on him like a two-dollar whore. His hands go up like he's under arrest and I'm grabbing his face to make out like our lives depend on this contact. He's obviously taken by surprise and I take advantage of that and shove my tongue in his mouth. Dylan moans . . . or grunts in alert, I can't tell which. I don't stop. His hard-on is hitting just the right spot and I'm a few seconds away from an orgasm, just from grinding. That in a nutshell says how freaking horny this pregnant woman is.

"Whoa, whoa, Andy. What are you doing?" Dylan slows my hips and my rising orgasm has diminished into the abyss. I look devastatingly at Dylan and just begin to cry. I needed that orgasm like my next breath. There's so much pent up lust, I'm about to burst. I was just denied release and now I'm a crying mess on this monster's lap.

"I need an orgasm so bad!" I wail. Dylan grips my chin and raises my head up to meet his gorgeous eyes. He looks startled and confused.

"What's going on, Andy? Talk to me." As if he didn't know!

"What's wrong? I'm horny as fuck and I need your dick to remedy the situation. I need it so bad." My voice cracks on the last word and I'm beyond mortified I'm practically begging him for his Johnson. The man has the guile to laugh at me. Seriously? I begin to push off him but, he grabs my forearms and keeps me in his lap.

"I don't mean to laugh. It's different to hear you wanting me so bad. Usually it's the other way around." He rubs my upper arms in a calming gesture.

"Why don't you want me?" I sniffle.

"Oh, baby. I want you so bad. I know it sounds stupid, but you have this little baby growing inside you. You're like this angel carrying my baby and I need to be delicate with you. You know how I am during sex. I'm not delicate. I'm really rough. I don't want to hurt you or the baby. You just make me so crazy sometimes when we're in the heat of the moment." He sighs and leans his forehead against mine. "Never doubt that I want you that way. I'll always want you that way."

I cradle his face and take in his sweet words. I completely understand where he's coming from. He is rough with me during sex and I love it. He would never hurt me or the baby. I'm just going to have to take matters in my own hands. "Do you trust me?" Dylan looks at me and nods. "Okay, take off your pants and I'll be right back."

"Baby, I don't think that's a good idea." I move off him. I'm not deterred. This is happening. He goes ahead and begins to unbutton his pants anyway. Good man. I come back from our bedroom and hide the item behind my back.

"Okay, now give me your hands." He holds out his hands like we're going to pray or something. He'll be praying for a reprieve that's for sure. I'm going to be riding this man till the sun comes up and it's time for me to go to work. I giggle to myself. This is going to be good. He'll be begging for mercy soon enough. I'm going to ring him of every bit of sperm in his body.

I quickly move the pink furry cuffs from around my back and click them together on his hands before he can realize what's going on. "Ugh, Andy. What are you doing?"

"What does it look like I'm doing? I'm going to ride you into next Tuesday and there's nothing you can do about it. Your hands are literally tied." I evil laugh and I think it scares Dylan. This is going to be fun. I pull off my panties and don't even bother to take off his shirt that I'm wearing. "Ready or not, here I come." I laugh.

Dylan seems pretty turned on and amped up for me to take over and give us what we both need. I pull out his cock from his boxers and he's ready to go. He's so hard and there's already precum dripping from his shaft. He needs this too. His dick seems mad that he's been denying his need. I'll make everything feel better.

I grab the middle of the cuffs and pin them behind his head against the seat cushion of the couch. "Damn, baby. This is so hot. Ride my dick." I sit in his lap, rubbing my wetness all over his aching cock. I was so close a few minutes ago, I bet I can come just from this friction. I bend down to kiss Dylan's lips. They're so soft, but our kiss is rough. Sliding back and forth on his cock feels incredible. My clit is getting the attention it needs.

"Dylan," I sigh. "I love your hard cock."

He groans loudly. There's tension in his arms and I realize his hands are in fists. Teasing him like this makes him even more aroused.

"Fuck, princess. I love it when you talk about my dick. You're so wet." His hips bump up to meet my grind. My head falls back as I concentrate on this connection. My aching pussy is about to erupt into a volcanic orgasm.

"I'm gonna come." I grip his arms that lie beside his head. My breathing hitches and then I scream. I might've blacked out. The next thing I know, I'm lying on Dylan's chest panting.

"Damn. That was so hot."

It's not over yet. Moving my hair away from my sticky

face, I give Dylan a satisfied smile. Bending down, I give him a sweet kiss.

Then, I'm on my knees lining myself over him. Slowly, I slide down his hardness just to torture us both. It's the most delicious feeling. "Fuck, you're so tight, angel." Oh, I like it when he calls me angel. It makes me feel precious. I grind against his pelvis and feel that sweet friction. I moan while Dylan grunts over my movements.

"Oh." It feels amazing. Slowly, I rise up and down tormenting us both with the slow rhythm. I revel in the feeling of us together again. The sensation is overwhelming. I want to be with this man. I really need him in my life. This man can completely destroy me and he has, but I keep coming back. There's nothing that can make me stay away. He's become so much to me. The man I once couldn't stand to be around has become my everything, the love of my life. I grip on to his shoulders tight as I ride him. My rhythm falters as I begin to feel the start of my orgasm take hold of me. Dylan can't help himself, he begins to pump his hips harder into me. I moan and grit my teeth as Dylan lets out a loud roar. We come at the same time, staring into each other's eyes. I kiss him fiercely. *I love you*, I don't say.

Birdie runs in checking on us. We're making a lot of noise. I love it. We needed this connection. Birdie sniffs around at our feet and loses interest. She trots on over to her piggy bed near the kitchen and lies down. Dylan is still inside me and not soft at all. I begin to grind against him again. He moans. Yes, we're both ready for round two. If there's anything I'm sure of it's Dylan's stamina. He can go hours. I'm betting on that tonight. I'm just getting started. The cuffs will be staying on for a while.

I know Dylan won't hurt me during sex. Truth is, he never has. Everything he's ever done in bed has been perfect and exactly what my body craves. I'll let him think he can't handle himself a little while longer while I have him cuffed. This whole scenario just makes this mating even more erotic. I can't wait to move this to the bedroom. I have a few ideas to make this even more fun, but at the moment I just need another orgasm and can't be bothered to change scenery.

The second time we make love that night is slow and sensual. We look into each other's eyes and it really does feel like love. He cradles my head and whispers dirty words in my ear. I grip on to him so hard. I never want to let go. We finally move into the bedroom and the cuffs come off and he holds me, cradling my small belly like we're the most precious things in the world.

15

*D*ylan seems nervous today. I don't know what's up with him, but he's been pacing all morning. It's Saturday, and he woke me up the usual way with his beard between my legs. It's my favorite. He woke me up pretty early too; I wonder what's on his mind. I wrap my hands around him from behind.

"What are you thinking about? You've been acting weird." He turns around and looks me up and down. "What do you think?" I twirl around in my pink cotton dress.

"I think you look beautiful." He seems a bit melancholy.

"So, where are we going this morning? Pancakes?" I ask excitedly. He shakes his head slowly. "Dylan, what's wrong? You're kinda freaking me out." He takes my hands in both of his.

"My mom wants to do brunch with us this morning." I pull away from his hands. His mother? He's never said a word about his parents. I thought they were both dead. Wait. This morning?

"What do you mean this morning? Why didn't you tell me? You just sprung this on me. I need to prepare. Oh my gosh. What the hell, Dylan? A girl has to prepare to meet the parents. I can't believe you . . . ugh!" I pace back and forth in the kitchen almost pulling my hair out. Why did I have to fall for a Neanderthal? He's so stupid!

"Andy. Andy, baby. It's . . ."

I point in his face. "If you're going to say that it's okay, I'm going to slap you!" He squeezes his lips shut. I'm freaking out. What if she doesn't like me? It took a while for Dylan to even warm up to me. Shit. This is a lot of pressure. She's going to be the grandmother to my child. I'm not ready for this right now.

"Andy, I can tell you're freaking out a little." I turn and give him a look that says I'm not freaking out a little. I'm freaking out a lot. "Look, my mom hates everyone. It doesn't matter. She's not like normal moms. It's just something we have to muddle through. She wanted to meet you since you're expecting her grandchild. It's probably just something she can talk to other old women about. It really doesn't matter." What the hell does that mean? She's not like other moms? Then a hear a sharp honk from outside. "Oh, that's her driver to come pick us up. Let's go." *Driver?*

Dylan grabs my arm and we head down to the car waiting for us. I'm so not ready for this. The driver opens the door for us. I'm expecting to see his mother in the backseat, but no one is there. Apparently, we're meeting her at a restaurant downtown. On the way Dylan informs me that his mom is rich as fuck and lives downtown. His father died a very long time ago, when he was only five. Nannies mostly raised him while his mother spent his father's money. She sounds like a cold woman. I feel bad for Dylan. It sounds like he didn't have anyone to love. Maybe that's why he's so afraid of it, because he's never had it before. The car stops and suddenly I'm looking up at the impressive Four Seasons Hotel. Dylan helps me out of the car. He rolls his eyes at the place and we bypass the doormen. I guess Dylan's been here before because he knows exactly where the dining area is.

The maître d' greets us at the entrance. "Elizabeth Ryder's party," Dylan announces his mom's name. I scout the area to see if I can see an older woman with a stick up her ass, but there's so many of them here, I can't figure out which one she is. I giggle to myself. The expensive dark marble floors stand out against the light color of the walls. The square wood tables are accented with colorful club chairs. The space is beautiful. I wish I could appreciate it more. My stomach is in knots. The host nods and we follow him to a small table near a window overlooking Chicago's towering buildings.

There's a woman who looks like she's had a lot of tightening done. It gives her a bit of a pinched look. Her dark brown hair is definitely not natural but her piercing eyes looks familiar. Her dainty wrinkled hand comes up for a kiss from Dylan. She has yet to acknowledge my presence.

"Dylan," her deep voice rumbles.

"Mother," Dylan replies, sounding more formal than I've ever heard him before. "This is Andrea Roberts." Andrea? Wow. This is more formal than I even imagined. I feel like I'm on an interview where I don't even want the job. She just nods in my direction and instructs us to sit with the wave of her hand. If she were a Disney character she would definitely be Maleficent. She gives me the willies. Dylan pulls my chair out and then sits down himself. I stay quiet, letting him have the lead on this.

Well, this chick gives off a superiority vibe. I'm surprised this is Dylan's mother.

"Now, what is this about you having a baby?" She sips on her teacup, awaiting Dylan's answer. From the sound of that question, she doesn't seem too pleased. It makes me sad.

If my mom were still alive, she'd be the most ecstatic grandmother ever. We'd go baby shopping, she'd help me design the nursery, and tell me how it was when she was pregnant with me. I miss her so much. Cancer sucks. She was the light in my life. While my father worked all the time, she dedicated her life to raising me. Then we received the news that she had lung cancer. It came as such a shock since she never smoked. She was gung ho about beating it and coming out the other side . . . except she didn't. She became increasingly worse. My father just buried himself in work more. I think he did love her in his own shitty way. I took care of her until her last day.

"Are you crying?" Dylan whispers in my ear. I quickly wipe away a tear I didn't even realize was there. I feel embarrassed. His mom is looking at me like I'm some piranha. She's absolutely horrified. It makes me laugh.

"Sorry, mood swings." I giggle as I wipe my cheek with a cloth napkin.

Elizabeth rings her hands in front of her seeming flustered. "Yes. Well, Dylan tells me your about five months pregnant now?" Oh. She's talking to me now?

"Yes. I have another sonogram next week. We should know the gender of the baby then." I smile, beaming at Dylan. He's been looking forward to seeing if we're having a girl or boy. We can't seem to agree on a name. I like fun names like Zander and Tootsie. Dylan said I have the worst taste in names. He likes Oliver or Beth. Which, now that I think of it, that's a deviation of his mom's name. What the hell?

"When can you tell if it's yours, Dylan?" Elizabeth replies. I'm stupefied. I'm sure my mouth is hanging open. Did that women just imply that I'm loose? What the actual fuck? Dylan squeezes my hand, but it does nothing to calm me down.

"Excuse me?" I grit through my teeth.

"Mother, I spoke to you about this. I know it's mine." I look incredulously at Dylan. He talked to her about this before? WHAT? I feel betrayed. He just threw me in shark infested waters with this woman and all I'm armed with is a floaty.

"Well, you never know these days." She shrugs as if she didn't just insult me. I stand up swiftly and throw my napkin down on the table.

"You know how he knows the baby is his? It's because

we fuck like rabbits. All. The. Time." Her mouth drops open and I make my way out of the restaurant. I mean seriously, who does she think she is? The Queen of Sheba? I'm out of here. I don't need this shit at five months pregnant. I need to be decorating a nursery and sitting on my ass playing video games.

I hail a taxi quickly. Dylan doesn't follow me out. I'm too pissed to deal with him either. What did he think would happen? I mean why even meet his mom if she's going to act like an entitled debutante? I use Dylan's credit card that he gave me for baby purchases and pay the taxi to go to his place so I can pick up Birdie. I need some time away from the Ryders.

Birdie is excited. She thinks we're going for a walk. We arrive back at my small studio a few minutes later. She plops down in the middle of the floor like she's throwing a tantrum. It makes me laugh. "Oh, Birdie. You're the only one I can count on. Do you know that?" I snuggle with her on the floor and cry silently. I'm so tired of this. I'm tired of being let down. I want someone to have my back, to look out for me. Dylan served me up on a silver platter to his mom.

If they spoke about paternity previously he should've known she would act like that. Why did he even introduce us? I need a partner who looks out for me. A man that really cares about me wouldn't have put me in that situation.

I get up and change into some comfy pajamas. I'm spending the rest of the day inside my modest studio. I don't want any more drama today unless it comes in the form of a Disney movie. A few minutes later, there's a knock on the door. Two guesses who that is. I huff and ignore it. Birdie, of course, hops on over to the door and squeals like the traitor she is.

"Come on, Andy. I know you're in there. I can hear Birdie." Yeah, she's practically humping the door to get to him. Well you can have him, girl. Crossing my arms, I settle in on the couch. I'm probably not acting very mature right now, but I'm so tired of feeling like trash. I want to be treated like a princess. Sounds funny now. "Andy, I'm tired of talking through the door. Please, open up."

I bound to the door and yell. "You're tired? I'm tired of being treated like crap. You knew your mom was going to be rude to me and you still brought me there. You didn't think about me at all. I love you and all you keep doing is hurting me. I'm so done!" My voice cracks and I begin to cry again.

"You love me?" Dylan whispers through the door as if he can't believe it.

I slide down to the floor. "Just leave, Dylan. I don't want to see you."

16

He doesn't leave immediately. He stakes out a few hours at my door, but then finally leaves before dinner. I'm relieved when he does. This is just too much stress during my pregnancy. I don't need this. I lie down and take a nap with Birdie for a while. I'm awoken sometime later by a light tapping at my door. I slowly get up and when I look through the peephole sure enough, there's Dylan.

"What do you want, Dylan?" I sound tired. I just want to crawl back in bed.

He raises up a bag of takeout. "I brought you some food. I knew you'd be hungry about this time. I wanted to check on you." Now he's concerned for my well-being?

"Look, Dylan. I don't appreciate you putting me in that position today. Takeout isn't going to smooth things over. I just want to be left alone." I begin to walk away from the door when he speaks up.

"I talked to her before we left to meet her. She

promised she was going to be on her best behavior. I wanted her to meet the mother of my child. I wanted . . . I don't know what I wanted. I thought for the first time she would be proud of me. I'm becoming a father. I own my own company. I bought out Johnson and Banks and now I'm expanding. I'm landing even bigger clients than they ever did."

"Wait. What? You were head of the hostile takeover of Johnson and Banks? You're the reason Cindy and I and everyone lost our jobs?" I gasp after that sentence. How could I be so obtuse? The same clients were there. I just thought they transferred with Dylan. I didn't think he would be capable of taking over the company. Everyone lost their jobs. He was there to swoop in and save the day. Offer me a job. It all makes sense. He kept this from me.

"Shit. Andy, I didn't mean for you to find out like this." Dylan bangs his head against the door.

I hit the door with my fist. "No. You didn't expect me to find out at all. Did you? You lying asshole! Cindy's been struggling since she lost her job. You heard me talk about her and you didn't feel guilty once? She has kids!" Tears stream down my face, but I'm so mad.

"Baby, I planned on hiring her when we got another office. You know that. I didn't mean for anyone to suffer—" I cut him off.

"Well, we did. All of us. Get the hell out of my building. I don't want to see you anymore!" With that I turn around and stomp toward my sleeping area causing Birdie to run under the bed. Plopping down on my bed, I hit my pillow a few times. I can still hear Dylan's muffled voice through the door. I ignore it and turn up *Beauty and the Beast*. Unfortunately, it's at the point in the movie when the beast is being a dick too. He yells at Belle and she flees. I can sympathize with her. Maybe I should just go back to Alabama? Different scenery might be good for a while. I look down under my bed and see a little pink snout peeking out from underneath it.

Poor Birdie. I didn't mean to scare her. She has no idea what's going on. She probably thinks I'm a madwoman. She has no idea what an asshole Dylan is. Just then, I feel a little flutter in my belly. Then there's a strong kick. "Ow! Oh my goodness." Cradling my stomach, I wait to feel more baby movements. This is such a special moment, I wish I could share it with someone. At least I don't feel completely alone anymore. I feel my little peanut moving around. I smile. "It's okay, baby. I'm going to take very good care of you. I can't wait to meet you, little one."

Fresh flowers are at my doorstep the following morning. The beautiful arrangement of roses brightens my kitchen nook area. I open the card and it reads:

Dear Andy,
I know you think I'm a monster right now. I'm
disappointed in myself too. I should've told you. Now, I'm
paying the price. I should've done a lot of things differently
with you. I'm sorry for every time I hurt you. I want to see
you. If you don't want to see me, I'll wait.
I'll wait forever for you, Andy Roberts.
Dylan

It's a nice gesture, but it doesn't explain anything. I look at that one sentence again, *I'll wait forever for you.* And sigh. Dylan can write a sweet note but I still haven't forgiven him for the multiple things he's done. Pinning the note to my bulletin board in my kitchen, I spend most of my Sunday folding clothes and watching movies.

Monday comes and goes and another bouquet of roses greets me when I get home from work. This one comes with a note as well. I take Birdie for a walk before I open it. By the time I get back, I'm on pins and needles. The note attached reads:

Dear Andy,
You're the first person to tell me that you love me. Did you know that? My father died when I was little and as you can see my mother isn't the type for sentiments like that. I'm still reeling from your declaration. I miss you terribly. I think of you and the baby all day, even Birdie.
I'll wait forever for you.
Dylan

For once, I feel I'm getting to know what his soul is like. It's sad. How could no one tell him they love him? I feel sorry for him. I know he's not looking for sympathy. He said it matter-of-fact but I can tell it bothers him. He probably doesn't know what to do with it either. Looking around to make sure no one's looking, I bring the note to my nose. It smells like him, that cinnamon smell. He's beginning to explain himself and that's good but I'm not ready to forgive and forget.

He kept that information from me about buying the company. I don't want a relationship with secrets. I need to be able to trust my partner. I want a strong foundation with someone. When I think about Dylan's and my relationship, it has crumbled at the seams. I pin his note to the board and fix myself and Birdie some dinner.

The week passes quickly. Each day I receive fresh flowers from Dylan. Every day he exposes his heart a little more to me. I wish we didn't have to do it through notes, but I appreciate seeing what he's going through and what he's been through. It definitely allows me to understand a few things about his behavior.

Dylan's sorry he didn't tell me about the buyout. He didn't want me to be deterred from working for him. He said he would've told me after he hired Cindy on. It reminds me to call Cindy.

"Hey. Did Dylan tell you I'm working for him now? He's paying me the big bucks." Cindy laughs over the phone. I'm shocked.

"No. He didn't tell me. There's a lot he doesn't tell me, apparently." I sit down at my kitchen table.

"Yeah, I started on Tuesday. He called me up over the weekend, said he found a new office and asked if I could start soon. I jumped at the chance. My old job just wasn't cutting it, as you know." Cindy seems so chipper and less stressed. It's good to hear her voice.

"Is he treating you right?" I tease.

"Oh, you know he is. He won't shut up about you and the baby. He's so gaga over you, sweetie. We need to have lunch soon. I gotta go. The kids need some dinner. They're like a pack of wolves. I'll talk to you later."

I hang up with Cindy and think about our conversation. Tomorrow's my appointment with the doctor. We're supposed to find out the sex of the baby. I wonder if Dylan will be there. Honestly, I'd be disappointed if he wasn't. I can't believe he gave Cindy a job. It makes me smile. Is he doing this for me or because it's the right thing to do? I guess time will tell.

17

It's finally Friday, appointment day. I've been excited all morning at work. A few of my colleagues have picked up on my mood. They have a pool going as to what sex the baby will be, it's fun. I really like my job. It's not like my old job, but it's different in a good way. The clock hits twelve and I'm off like a prom dress.

I walk to the L and get on. It's faster than an Uber would be. I can't wait to hear whether I'm having a girl or a boy. I'm sitting in a seat thinking about baby names when my cell phone rings from my purse. I quickly scramble for the phone and see that my dad's calling me. That's a first. I answer before it goes to voicemail.

"Hello?" I know I must sound confused. This isn't the best place to have a conversation with my father. It's rather noisy on the train. I plug one of my ears to hear better.

"Hello, Andy. It's your father." I roll my eyes. Yeah, he would have to tell me it's him.

"Hello." This is awkward. I haven't told him I'm

pregnant yet and we usually only call on holidays just to say Merry Christmas and then we both hastily hang up. I don't want to say my dad is a bad guy. He just wasn't ever there. He's like a stranger I'm related to. He's handsome and charismatic around other people, especially people he works with, but at home he couldn't be bothered with me. It's like it wasn't his decision to become a father. We've never talked about our strained relationship if you can even call it a relationship.

"I just wanted to call to tell you I'm getting married." My mouth drops open. What the hell? Am I in a *Twilight Zone* episode? Am I being punk'd right now? My father doesn't have a loving bone in his body. Who would he marry? He's too involved in himself to care about anyone else. If my dad was a Disney character he would definitely be Gaston. "Andy, are you there?"

"Yup." I'm pretty much speechless as this point. I have no words. What the hell do I say to that? "Umm, congratulations?" It sounds like a question because I can't believe this is real. Maybe I'm still sleeping in my bed right now. Yeah, I never got up, I'm snuggled in bed with Birdie. I pinch myself. *Ow!* Nope, I'm definitely on the L with a bunch of smelly people going to the doctor.

"Well, I'm in Chicago and I would like to have dinner to finalize everything. Are you free tonight?" Finalize everything? He's here in Chicago?

"Umm, no I don't have dinner plans. What do you mean finalize?" He clears his throat over the phone.

"Well, I would like you to come to the wedding. I'm getting married here in Chicago. She's still arranging things and we need to get everything set up. So, how about we have dinner tonight at seven?" My father is getting married here in Chicago and he wants me to come to the wedding? This whole scenario is so bizarre. I guess it would be a good time to tell him in person that I'm pregnant. We need to hash out some things and I need to meet this woman I guess.

"Okay, how about seven at Pequod's? They have the best deep-dish pizza." I've seriously been craving this pizza for over a week. Their pizza is amazing. It's like a religion there, very sacred. They have their priorities straight that's for sure. My father grunts, but then acquiesces. It's not his scene. He'd rather go to a fine Italian restaurant. Well, too bad. I'm pregnant and I want what I want. He'll thank me later when he tries the pizza.

We say our goodbyes as the train comes to my stop. This doctor's appointment should be interesting. Dylan and I are still on the outs and my mood swings are driving me crazy. I'm missing and loving Dylan and then I'm hating and cursing his Prince of Darkness ways. He's trying though. I get fresh flowers every day with a peek into his mind. He's never been forthcoming when it comes to his feelings, but when he writes me those notes I feel like I'm getting to know him better. I get a little peek into his soul.

I just don't know what to do about us right now. I'd like us to be together and I want to be a family. That just might be something Dylan isn't capable of. He continues to keep things from me and he still has a wall up. Except with those notes. I feel the wall coming down brick by brick. He's trying for me. Maybe he would like to meet my dad? That would show me he's serious about this. I met his mom, it would only make sense. Yes, I'll ask him at the appointment, if he shows.

Arriving at the doctor, I don't see Dylan in the waiting room. I go through the normal weigh in and blood pressure. I can't wait to find out if we're having a girl or boy. There's a light knock on the door. "Come in," I call out. Then, there he is. Dylan peeks in and smiles when he sees me up on the examination table. He's wearing his usual attire of jeans and a dark T-shirt. This man doesn't even have to try to look good.

"Hey." He rushes over to me and gives me a strong hug. I hug him back and smell that wonderful cinnamon scent.

"Hi." I'm so glad he's here. I've really missed him. I know it was me pushing him away, but I just can't take much more of him withdrawing or keeping things from me. Dylan pulls back and cups my face. His eyes are asking. I nod in response. His eyes light up and then his lips are on mine. I grip onto his black shirt as my legs wrap around his waist, pulling him toward me. His moan kills me.

I forget we're in a doctor's office and make out with him like we're at home. My hands run through his hair as his tongue probes my mouth. I open for him as his hands grip my sides. His face pulls away slightly.

"Andy, I've missed you so much."

"Shhh, less talking. More kissing." I bring his mouth back down to mine. He chuckles but obliges. I needed this so bad, this connection with him. I've missed him as well. I want us to be together. We're better together than we are apart. We can totally master this parenting thing. Dylan pulls back quickly and then comes in for one big smacking kiss.

"Did you get my flowers and my notes?" I nod. "I really need to talk to you. Can I take you home after the appointment?" His forehead rests against mine, his eyes pleading.

"Yes. I would like to talk to you too."

He smiles and peppers my face with kisses. I giggle and fan him away. Our doctor arrives shortly after and we move to another room where the sonogram machine is. Dylan and I are so giddy we can't stand still. I don't care if it's a boy or a girl, I'm just excited to know. I'm a planner; I need to plan out the nursery, baby clothes, and toys.

"Now, it's time for the big question. Would you like to know the sex of your baby?" My doctor looks to us as her hand lingers on the strange nozzle laying on my stomach. Dylan and I both say yes at the same time. The doctor laughs. "It's a girl!" Grinning ear to ear, I can't contain my excitement for this little girl growing inside me. We will have tea parties and I can decorate a pink nursery! We'll make cookies in the kitchen and I'll take her to the park. While I'm planning all the things I'd like to do with my little girl, Dylan squeezes my hand.

He leans his forehead against my temple. "Pink everywhere." I belly laugh at his comment. Yes, there will be pink everywhere. "I can't wait," he adds. Tears stream down my face as he kisses me sweetly on the lips.

18

We drive back to my place in relative silence. We're both taking in the news of this little girl. I couldn't help smiling and rubbing my belly. A couple of times Dylan reached over and petted my stomach. It's such a sweet gesture. I feel like we're on the same page now and in a good place.

When we get to my apartment, I decide Birdie needs a walk. Dylan suggests we go to Montrose Dog Beach. I've never taken her there, but I can't wait to see how she reacts to the sand and water.

Dylan and I take a romantic stroll on the beach with my little pink pig. With the Chicago skyline behind us, we talk about our future ahead of us. "Andy, I hope you know by the flowers and the notes that I only want to be with you. I want you to move back in with me. I want to wake up to you every morning and make love to you every night. Ever since you told me you loved me, I've been in a tailspin. I can't sleep. I can't work. I can only think about you. I've realized I'm in love with you too."

I stop in my tracks. I've waited to hear those words from him. I almost can't believe what I hear. Dylan walks ahead of me and then turns around, holding my hands in his. Birdie sits at my feet, reveling in the sand. He steps closer and moves his hands to the back of my head. "I love you, Andy Roberts." Tearing up, I close my eyes to soak in this moment. When I open them, he's waiting for my reaction. His eyes are pleading. I'll put him out of his misery.

"I love you, Dylan Ryder." He rushes to kiss me. His beard tickles my face, I've missed that. I wrap my arms around his neck and rise up on my tiptoes to deepen the kiss. I'm so elated. I might've waited forever for this man to come to the conclusion that he loves me. I'm just glad he's smart enough to figure it out now. "Will you come meet my dad? He's in town and wants to meet with me. Apparently, he's getting married." I blow out a breath.

Dylan's reaction is reserved. "Yeah, I'll be there for you. Does he know about the baby?"

"Nope." I shake my head.

"This should be interesting." He kisses my forehead. "Do you get along with your dad?"

"Sure, I guess. Can't really fight with someone who's never there." Dylan nods and grips my hand tighter.

"I'm glad we're doing this. We should tell him you're expecting together. Do you think he'll be excited to be a grandfather?" I shrug my shoulders. Who knows.

"Probably not. He wanted me set in my career. He

doesn't really hold personal relationships very high, obviously. He's all about work and making something of yourself. It's sad really. I'm the total opposite, I think family is everything."

Dylan looks off into the distance. I shake his arm to bring him back to me. I give him a bright smile to let him know we're together in this. He returns my smile and we move on down the beach. Our little family of four, Dylan, Birdie, our baby, and I.

∼

We arrive at the quaint brick building at seven on the dot, walking hand in hand. The bar greets us on the right and small booths and tables flank the other side of the space. We make our way to the back where I see my dad's salt and pepper hair. I know this isn't his type of place, but it's definitely Dylan and I's. Before I get to the table my father rises up and meets us with a smile, which slowly turns into a frown. He looks down at my stomach and then points. "What is that?"

Oh, boy. This isn't going to go smoothly at all I'm afraid. We haven't even made it to the table. Dylan steps up and extends his hand. My father takes it without thinking. "Hi, sir. I'm Dylan. Andy is carrying our baby girl. She's due in June. Congratulations! You're going to be a grandfather." Well, that's getting it all out there on the table. My dad looks between us in shock. He's not saying anything. Dylan motions us to step over to the table my dad just vacated. That's when I see who's sitting at my father's table. It's none other than Mrs. Ryder, Dylan's mother.

"Dylan?" I look to him to see if he is hallucinating the horrendous monster as well. He looks as confused as I do.

"Mother?" She looks completely put out in this restaurant. Her face shows she's not happy to be here either. It almost makes me smile, but then I remember I'm still in the same room with this woman.

"Mother?" My father finally speaks up and acknowledges the elephant in the room. Or should I say Maleficent? "This is my fiancée, Elizabeth Ryder," my father replies.

Dylan and I both look at each other. I freeze in complete horror. What the actual fuck? Oh, hells no! My dad is marrying his mother? That would make us, stepbrother and stepsister? How in the hell is this my reality right now?

"Fuck."

"What did you say, young lady?" Oops. I must've said that out loud. "And what is this with you being pregnant?"

Dylan takes a seat across from his mom and pulls out a seat for me. I sit down since I feel like fainting. This cannot be happening. For the first time in my life I feel like putting my dad in time-out. Does he not see how fucked-up this situation is? What are the odds?

"Dad, I'm pregnant. I'm almost six months and . . ." I grab Dylan's hand for support. He nods. "We're having a baby girl. Now, what are you doing with Dylan's mother?" My father seems taken aback with my frankness. He hasn't been around me in a long time, he doesn't know how much

I've grown up in the past three years here in Chicago. It's not like he ever visited me, until now.

"Elizabeth and I met on a cruise a couple of months back. I was working on my laptop at one of the tables and she and I happened to sit at the same one. We ate together every night after that. We're getting married next week." My dad acts like this is the most normal thing in the world. I've never wanted to punch him, until now. Only he would find the worst woman in the world and want to marry her.

"What?" Dylan yells out. I'm glad he's freaking out about this too. "Why didn't you tell me any of this, Mother?" His mom picks at the ice in her water cup like there's dirt in it. Just watching her judgmental face makes me nauseous. Hmm, maybe if I threw up on her she wouldn't marry my dad? She'd be disgusted with my whole family because of it. I smile to myself. I'm in my own world when I hear his mom's reply.

"Not that I need to answer to you, Dylan, but I was going to tell you when we had brunch last. That is until you were rude to me and then rushed out of the Four Seasons. I figured I'd get in touch with you before the wedding. Send you a formal invitation." She dusts off her lap like there's errant dust bunnies in the pizza place. I hate how she talks to Dylan. She acts like she's not even related to him.

My dad just sits back like this is a completely legitimate way to speak to your child. The more I think about it, the more it actually does make sense. They totally deserve each other. I turn to look at Dylan and he still seems gobsmacked. I'm thinking about getting my deep-dish pizza to go. At that moment I feel a little movement in my stomach. My little girl is making her presence known at this crazy moment in time.

I grab Dylan's hand from his lap and place it on my belly. I can see the anger diminish from his face as he turns to look at my stomach moving under his hand. This little moment has given us a reprieve from the ridiculous situation we find ourselves in. Dylan's gorgeous brown eyes look into mine and he smiles brilliantly at me. "Let's get outta here." In that moment, I think we both realize our parents are better off without us. They can rot with each other for all I care. I have Dylan and this little family that we're making. It will be nothing like our parents because we are nothing like them. I return his smile and stand up from my chair.

"Let's blow this popsicle stand," I crow.

"Mom, send us the invite in the mail. Maybe I'll see you around." Dylan seems determined as he leads me out of the restaurant.

"Andy?" My dad calls to my retreating backside. I don't answer and we stop at the bar and grab me a deep-dish pizza to go. They're the best in the city and I'm not going to let Maleficent or Gaston ruin my pizza time. We make it back to Dylan's loft while the pizza's still hot.

"Can you believe that shitstorm?" He plops down on the couch shaking his head. "How in the hell did our parents find each other? Do you think they've done it? I might be sick. Ugh." His head falls back against the couch in dismay.

I pet Birdie and make my way over to him. "I doubt

it. I think they're just doing it for companionship or maybe money. I think they deserve each other." I sit down next to him. He places his hand on my belly. The entire way home he kept rubbing my belly, it was adorable. I know he's waiting for another kick from the baby.

Dylan moves to the floor in front of me and holds my belly like a trophy between his large hands. "Hey, baby girl." Dylan's talking to our peanut. My hands go to his hair as he continues to talk to our baby. "I'm your daddy. I make mistakes sometimes with your mom, but I love her more than anything. And I already love you too." Crocodile tears are falling in his hair at this point. He's so sweet. It's so endearing hearing him speak to our baby like this. I know he's going to be a great father. We're going to be a little family. He already pampers Birdie, I can't wait to see how Dylan is with our little girl. He kisses my belly and stands up.

"Come here. I want to show you something." Dylan pulls me to my feet and I follow him into his bedroom. I think I've already seen what he's about to show me. I giggle to myself. Then, he surprises me again. There at the end of his bed is a crib. It's a beautiful wood crib put together and ready for a little bundle. I grip on to his forearm for support.

"You did this?" I go over to the beautiful crib and hold onto the railing. It's perfect. It's a simple maple wood crib with clean lines. I couldn't have picked out a better one. "I love it." I rush to him and give him the biggest hug. "I can't believe you did this. I haven't even been able to think about baby items yet. I've been working and saving. This means so much, Dylan."

"I couldn't stop thinking about you and the baby." He sits on the bed and leans back on his hands. "You look so beautiful." I blush at his compliment.

"You gone soft on me, Prince of Darkness? What else did you do with your hands while I was gone?" I smirk at him.

He shakes his head at me. "Have you been touching yourself, baby? Thinking about me in bed at night?" He lies back on the bed and rubs against the zipper of his jeans. He's just asking for me to crawl on top of him.

"Maybe." I leave it at that. I move to straddle him.

"The real question is, what are you going to do about it?"

I glance down at his crotch and giggle.

Dylan roars with laughter and then rolls me delicately on my back. "I think you know, baby." He grinds his hips against mine and I feel that sweet friction. He slides off the bed. Dylan slips off my leggings and then slowly pulls my panties down. "Are you ready for my mouth? I need to take my time with this pussy."

I moan. Suddenly he stands up and moves to the nightstand. What is he up to? Dylan pulls out the vibrator. What in the hell? He smiles as he kneels between my legs again. I sit up on my elbows and watch him.

"Are you going to use that vibrator on me?" I sound breathless.

"Yes, baby. I'm gonna make you feel so good." I feel his lips on my core, sweet light kisses. I sigh and open my legs wider. I have no shame. I need this. I want this. I grip his hair as his lips move to my clit. My hips move back and forth on their own accord. I need the friction. Dylan's being so delicate it's driving me crazy.

"Dylan," I moan. He sucks hard on my clit and then an orgasm slams into me out of nowhere. "Yes. Yes!" I bite down on my knuckle to bear the onslaught of adrenaline rushing through my body. I'm shivering and he's still licking me like a lollipop. Click. The vibrator clicks on. I'm not even over this orgasm yet and he's already upping the sensations. He places the vibrator over my clit and leaves it there.

"You like that, princess?" He wipes his mouth off with one hand. Dylan kisses the inside of my thigh and then I feel his fingers.

"Oh God, yes," I moan. That vibrator and his fingers are going to kill me. Whoa. It feels intense. I can hear how wet I am for him. "Dylan, I can't take it anymore." All these movements are too much, I can't concentrate on one. It's like everything is coming at me at once and I don't know how to deal except have another orgasm.

"You're just going to have to, puddin' pop." Dylan smiles.

I begin to giggle and then another orgasm rises up and takes hold of me. I grip the blanket beneath me and thrash my head back and forth. Dylan has to hold me down. My legs jerk and convulse. I squeeze my eyes shut as light hits the back of my eyelids. It's like fireworks. Then it's dark and all I can hear is my heavy breathing. The blackness recedes. I wake to Dylan above me. He kisses my lips sweetly and I grab his back and pull him down to me. He's careful of my belly.

"You trying to kill me, Prince of Darkness?" I nibble on his neck. Deciding he's wearing too many clothes, I grab at his dress shirt and begin unbuttoning.

"No, I'm just trying to love you." That sweet sentiment just makes me hornier. "Shit, woman, that feels good." I rake my nails down his back once I have his shirt open. Dylan throws his shirt off and scoots off the bed to remove his jeans.

I'm a little hesitant to remove my shirt. I have a big belly now, and even though I think it's a beautiful thing, I'm not sure how Dylan will see it. My belly button looks weird and I have stretch marks on my abdomen. Dylan senses my hesitation.

"Show me, baby." I hesitate on the hem, feeling its soft texture. I look away. Dylan leans over me and trails kisses down my neck. "I think you're the most beautiful woman I've ever seen." He licks my collarbone.

"Yeah, well . . . my shirt's not off yet," I grumble. I know I'm being petulant, but I'm feeling insecure and he still looks hot as hell. Moving his hand to my shirt, he slowly pulls it up over my tummy. His lips descend and he peppers light kisses all over my abdomen. It makes me giggle.

"I love your body. It's so precious and it's carrying my child. What could be sexier than that?" He pulls my shirt off the rest of the way and removes my bra. I'm completely naked on the bed. "I want you so bad right now."

I pull him down to me. He braces himself above me.

"Then show me," I demand. His movements become quicker and his kisses become a little crazed, like he doesn't know where to start. It's cute and frustrating at the same time. "Give it to me, Dylan," I whine. My body fidgets underneath him.

"Gladly, princess." His husky voice fans across my neck. Dylan fits between my legs and rubs on one hip. "I got you, sweetie." He rubs his cock between my folds gently. I raise my hips to get more friction. He's teasing me. I huff. Dylan gives me that same smirk that used to piss me off, but now I love. Maybe we always loved each other and we just fought because we didn't know how to express it. I'd like to think that we were always destined to be together.

He cups my cheek as he slides in slowly. "Fuck, you're so wet." Dylan begins to pump in earnest. "I'm going to make you come so hard you'll never doubt my love for your body, princess." His body towers over mine as he ruts inside me relentlessly. I love every moment of it. I tell him harder, faster, don't stop. My loud moans bounce off the walls of his loft. Dylan loves it when I'm loud. I definitely couldn't shut up if my life depended on it right now.

"That's right. Tell the neighbors what I'm doing to you." His hair flops in his face and a light sheen of sweet glistens his cheeks. He's so gorgeous. I pull his face down to feel his beard against my skin. His cinnamon scent wraps me like a warm blanket. I can't imagine being with another man. This is who I want to be with always. I begin to cry like usual. Dylan just smiles and wipes my tears as he slows a little. His lips meet mine and his tongue slips between us.

"I love you." I sniffle. His brown eyes look into mine.

"I know," he replies. I laugh.

"Am I the Princess Leia to your Han Solo?" His forehead rests on mine.

"No. I don't think Han ever fucked Leia like this." Dylan moves me so I'm lying on my side. He lifts one leg and his hips piston against my ass hitting my G-spot. My hand moves to his abs as my other grips the blanket.

"Oh, Oh. Holy shit," I scream. He grabs my hands and pulls them over my head as my orgasm takes hold of my body. He doesn't slow. He continues to fuck me into the bed.

"Yes! I love you." Dylan's orgasm breaks free and coats my inner walls in his seed. Aftershock orgasms hit me like Morse code and exhaust my body. He's heaving out deep breaths above me. Tired and spent, Dylan lies behind me cradling my extended belly, always cradling. I hold his hand against me, intertwining our fingers.

"I love you too," I say dreamily.

19

"I think you should quit," Dylan says as I'm sitting at my old desk looking over the mess that he's made over the past few months. I shake my head.

"You just want me to clean up this pile of paperwork." I snicker at him. He pushes off the couch and approaches me.

He rubs my shoulders, trying to butter me up no doubt. "I miss you. I miss our lunches together and being able to blow off some steam by playing video games with you. I miss seeing you working at that desk . . . and what we did on that desk." He winks at me. I blush and turn away. He still has the ability to frazzle me.

"Yeah, but you moved the office already and have Cindy working for you, so it would be different anyway." I change the subject. "Do you want a grilled cheese or something?" I move to the kitchen.

"No. I want you on your desk," he says grumpily. I make an overexaggerated pouty face at him. He laughs and the discussion is forgotten. I would like to work for him again, I'm just not sure if spending that much time together is a good idea. We'd probably get tired of each other and I want this relationship to last and have a family with him.

I think about those fun days when we used to work together. It seems so long ago now. So much has changed. Gone are the days of hooking up with no strings, no labels. A baby complicates everything. Parents complicate everything. I drum my fingers on the kitchen counter waiting for the toast to pop.

I think about last night's fiasco pizza dinner. I still can't believe our parents are getting married. What are the odds of them both being on the same cruise at the same time? My father working on a cruise sounds about right though.

"What are you thinking about?" Dylan sidles up behind me and kisses me on the cheek.

"How crazy our parents are," I mumble. He sighs heavily behind me.

"Yeah. What are we going to tell them when they find out their kids procreated and it resulted in an unplanned pregnancy?" Dylan says sarcastically as he chuckles against my neck.

"Yeah, I think they already know that, you caveman." I giggle. I like it when he's in a good mood like this. He's almost playful. He's not taking anything too seriously and it makes me want to react the same way. Like water off a duck's back.

"Shit. I guess we'll just have to disown them." He chuckles. "Honestly Andy, they were never in our lives to begin with. Why should we be in theirs? I won't go to the wedding . . . if it comes to that."

"You don't think they'll get married?"

He shakes his head in response. "Do you think those two could live together for even a week? I don't think anyone can live with my mother. It won't last, but this will." He holds my hand in his. I close my eyes and feel his body against my back and his arms wrapped around me. Yeah. This is what love feels like. This is what a family feels like. "Your toast is getting cold in the toaster. It popped out a few minutes ago."

I turn and smile at him. "I love you."

Dylan kisses my nose and I finish making my grilled cheese. All feels right with the world again.

A week passes and we don't receive any invitation. We look at that as a win. There's no announcement in the paper either. Dylan said his mom would put it in print if she got married. I guess that fell through then. No stepsiblings for us. Although, Dylan got off on messing with me by calling me his stepsister.

I've been thinking about Dylan's comment over and over again about me working for him. It's nagging at the back of my mind. I can't stop thinking about it. I'd really love for us to work together again and work with Cindy like we talked about before. I decide to broach the subject with him after dinner one night.

"Baby?" I bite my lip and wait for him to look up from his phone.

"Princess?" I love it when he calls me that. I know I'm the only one he's called that and it makes me all warm inside. Dylan looks up when I don't say anything. I want his undivided attention.

"I'm thinking of maybe coming back to work for you." His eyes light up. "I have a condition though." Dylan folds his hands in front of him. I feel like we're in a business meeting. I put on my poker face and proceed with my request. "I'd like a pink stapler." I laugh.

"Done." Dylan gets up from the table and makes his way toward me. "I think I need to interview you for the position though. It's very strenuous and you'll be glued to your desk. You may even have to work through lunch. I'll need someone who is hands on. Who obeys my every command. Someone who will bend over at my will." I giggle at all his innuendoes. "In fact, I'd like to take you through a few positions right now."

I move away and to my phone. "Oh, I can't wait to tell Cindy!" I dial her number quickly.

"Ugh!" Dylan groans. He totally thought he was getting laid right now. He probably will in a minute, but I want to share the good news with Cindy first. It's going to be like old times, all of us working together. Except, Dylan and I might actually get along. I laugh to myself. I'm so proud that Dylan is doing so well and is able to hire us back on. I'm looking forward to seeing the new office. We're soon to be an office of five, Dylan, Birdie, the baby, Cindy, and I.

Cindy is ecstatic and can't wait for me to start working for the P. Revere accounting firm. Dylan takes me to the new office which is just a couple of blocks away from his place. Things move fast after that. I set up my new desk and organize my space. Dylan is over the moon and working hard to make this new location work for all of us. Birdie even has her own space next to my desk. She still prefers messing around in Dylan's office though.

Before we can say Swingline stapler, we're all settled in our roles and new routine. Cindy helps Dylan with the smaller accounts and I handle the office. Dylan and I are still able to get away for lunch occasionally. We go back to his loft and hump like bunnies. Cindy is probably on to us. She smirks every time we arrive back from one of our romps. I like being naughty with Dylan.

Soon, it's a month until I'm due. Cindy has been giving me great advice over the past few weeks. She even bought a few gifts for the baby. Dylan and I have gotten all the staples like bottles, bibs, burp cloths, onesies, a carrier, and a stroller. I've pinked out Dylan's loft with all things baby. He hasn't even batted an eye at the pink overload. He's officially joined the pink side. Another point for Team Pink!

We decided it was best to let my lease up on my small studio apartment. We've officially moved in together. Which is good because when this baby comes she'll be waking him up too. It's just like any other Friday in our small office, when Dylan asks me out to lunch. I'm giddy because between the move, the new office, and our baby growing inside me, I've been completely exhausted. I've been passing out on Dylan frequently, which means there hasn't been much hanky panky. My lady bits are in great need of Dylan's family jewels.

"Bye, Cindy. We're off." She winks at me while she

speaks on the phone. Dylan leads me out. We're not two seconds out the door before I'm kissing him.

"Andy." Dylan seems surprised. I stick my tongue in his mouth to shut him up. My hand moves down to his crotch and just like that he's hard. I smile in our kiss.

"I knew you were hard for me. I can't wait to get to your place." Dylan moves my hand from his crotch.

"Princess, I wanted to take you out today." He holds both my hands in his and brings them to his lips. I've just been cock blocked by my own cock. This is different. Maybe we're going to do it after lunch. Well, at least I'm getting food. We get into Dylan's car which is odd. Normally we walk to a place or eat something at his loft.

"Where are we going?" I ask while we're driving on Lake Shore Drive. It's May in Chicago and I'm enjoying the sun.

"You'll see. We should be there soon." He's been really quiet, but it's nice to just be together alone enjoying this wonderful day. Lake Michigan is on our left as we head south. I have no idea where we are going. We haven't traveled this far for lunch before. Soon we turn onto East Grand Avenue.

"Here we are. I've never taken you to Navy Pier and I figured since you're from Alabama you probably didn't venture here yet." I gawk at the massive entrance to the Pier. It's one of the coolest things I've ever seen. I feel like a little kid. There's a massive Ferris wheel, restaurants, and yachts parked in the new transient docks. We are lucky enough to get a parking spot. He grabs my hand like he's antsy to get someplace. Dylan must be hungrier than I am. I just can't get over the magnitude of this place.

We sit down at a seafood place that's known for their crabs apparently. I order a hot dog there. Dylan laughs at my order. It's a pretty expensive place too. We eat until we're both stuffed.

"This was so nice to get out. I guess we better head back before Cindy wonders if we left her to do all the work."

Dylan smiles at me and looks up at the Centennial wheel in front of us. "How about we go for a spin?"

My nose crinkles up as I grin at the monstrosity. "Really?" My tattooed hipster bearded boyfriend wants to take me on a Ferris wheel ride? Dylan grabs my hand and leads me to it.

"Yeah, why not?" I shrug my shoulders and follow his lead. This should be a lot of fun. We'll have a great view of Downtown and Lake Michigan.

The wait's not too long since it's lunchtime and soon we are rising up in the air, two hundred feet in the air to be exact. Good thing I'm not afraid of heights. I feel like I'm in high school again and I'm on an afternoon date with my boyfriend, which I guess I am. That thought makes me happy.

We're living our own life together and soon we'll be celebrating a birth. Just one more month. I can't wait to hold this little girl in my arms. Dylan will totally be one of those sexy dads. I bite my lip thinking about him with a baby carrier. Yup. Total hottie.

"What are you thinking about, sweetie?" Dylan

brushes my bangs away from my eyes and leans in for a kiss. He's being so romantic, a wonderful drive to a nice lunch and then a ride on the Centennial wheel.

"I'm thinking about what a nice day it is. What are you thinking about?" I turn away from the marvelous view and gaze at my gorgeous boyfriend. He holds my hand and looks into my eyes.

"I'm thinking how I could hold a girl like you. How lucky I am that you're having my baby and I want to wake up with you next to me every morning. I'm my best self when I'm with you. I want to be a better man because of you. You're like this light in my life I can't help but gravitate toward. I just want to bask in your glow forever." I blink a couple of times.

"You were thinking about a lot." I don't know what else to say. He chuckles and reaches in his pocket. I don't see what he pulls out because his other hand pulls up his shirt. His tight abs greet me and I sigh. I look around and try and pull his shirt back down. No one but me needs to see that. He laughs but pulls his shirt up to show me his pecs. That's when I notice a new tattoo I haven't seen before.

"I got it this morning during that meeting I told you I had to go to." He laughs. "It should be bandaged but I couldn't wait to show you."

I reach my hand out. "Is it still tender?" I want to touch it so bad.

"No. Touch me, baby." I smile and gingerly caress the new mark. Where once there was a small gap of untouched skin, now the name Andy sits just above his heart. The script is beautiful and a bit of a contrast to the other tattoos on his chest. Most are images. Mine is the only name.

"Dylan." I grab his face and kiss him hard. "I can't believe you did that." I feel like we're on top of the world here and nothing can touch us. I mean, my boyfriend tattooed my name across his chest. Now, that's commitment.

Dylan brings my face close to his and whispers, "Will you marry me, Andy?" That's when he opens his hand and I see a black velvet box. My mouth hangs open. He opens the small box and I see a pink princess cut stone in a gold band. I gasp. It's absolutely gorgeous. "You'll always be my princess."

I can't speak. I just nod my answer as he slides the ring on my shaky hand.

When I'm finally able to form words, I say, "I love you. Yes, of course I'll marry you." Dylan just laughs at me and wipes my tears and holds me like he's never going to let go.

"I love you, princess."

20

*D*ylan expected me to want a big ceremony, but I just wanted us to be together. I may like pink pretty things, but I really don't need much. When the man of my dreams asks me to marry him I want to get on with it.

We had a civil ceremony at the courthouse downtown two weeks later with Cindy and Dylan's phone buddy Sam in attendance. I wore a pink empire waist dress that stopped at my knees. I couldn't help myself. It had to be pink. I looked like a pink balloon, but I was happy. Dylan was handsome in one of his tailored suits. Sadly, Birdie couldn't be there.

We had an amazing reception though. We all went back to the Navy Pier and rode some rides. Cindy brought her kids and even Sam came along. He's a bit of a workaholic, but we're working on loosening him up. He needs to let go every once in a while.

Now, I'm happily married and overdue for a baby girl by three days. "Come out!"

Dylan chuckles at my outburst. "She'll come anytime now. We're on her clock." He rubs my aching feet and I fall even more for this man. He's so sweet and considerate. Who knew that the man who drove me insane at work a year ago would be my husband and the father of my child today.

"Let's have sex. The doctor said that could help." I smile devilishly.

Dylan gives me a grimace. "You know I want you, but the baby is right there . . . it's a little weird, sweetie."

"Ugh!" I throw my hands up in the air. "I can't even get sex!" And then my water breaks!

"See!" Dylan motions to my current condition. "I knew it." He laughs. "I guess you were ready to pop."

I give him a look that makes him slither into the bedroom to get my hospital bag without another word. I call Cindy in the meantime to see if she can care for Birdie while I'm gone. I leave a key for her under the mat and then we're on our way to the hospital. As Dylan exits the elevator the strap to my hospital bag trips him up and he face-plants on the lobby floor. I cringe as he just lies there.

"Oh, are you okay?" I try to reach down to comfort him but a contraction comes and I let out a wail across the lobby. Dylan turns over onto his back.

"I think I might have broken my ankle." I look down and see his right ankle is starting to swell. I bend down to help him up after my contraction eases.

"Well, good thing we're going to the hospital, right?" I

try and laugh it off. I hope he didn't really break it. That would be horrible right now. I need my husband at my side for this birth.

"Uh, Andy?" I wrap his arm around my shoulder as we hobble out to the car.

"This is my right foot. You know the one I have to drive with." I look down again and sure enough, he's right. Shit.

"No problem, I'll drive." I smile triumphantly.

"No. No, Andy. Just . . . no. You're in labor right now. You don't need to be driving a large machine. That's not very smart. We'll just call a taxi or get an Uber." Dylan shakes his head emphatically.

"Baby, by the time an Uber or taxi got here, we'd already be at the hospital." Another contraction comes and I squeeze Dylan's wrist hard. I take deep breaths to concentrate on relaxing. Although I don't feel like this breathing is doing shit. If anything, it's making me angrier. Those liars at the Lamaze class! After the contraction decreases, I begin to move out of the lobby.

"Oh my God, woman! You're impossible. What happens if you have a contraction on the road?"

I bat my eyelashes at him. "Then I'll just pull over. It's really not that big of a deal. I read once where a woman was driving on the freeway and delivered her own baby. I can at least drive to a hospital that's like ten minutes away. If it gets too intense then I'll pull over. Easy peasy lemon squeezy."

Dylan groans and tries to step down on his hurt ankle. "Fuck. There's no way I can drive with this pain."

This guy wants to talk about pain right now, *really*? I feel like smacking him. *Okay, let's do this*.

We argue a few more minutes outside of the car until I go almost exorcist on him and then he complies and gets into the passenger side. I wait until I have another contraction to drive, so I'll have a good break to drive in. Dylan looks helpless in the passenger seat. I'm feeling like Wonder Woman right now. I'm in labor driving myself and my injured husband to the hospital.

Everything is smooth sailing until we get about halfway there and a contraction hits me. It causes me to gun the car a little and speed. Dylan freaks out and flails his hands in the air while I try and concentrate on slowing down on the accelerator.

"It's okay, I got this." I breathe and it helps to focus on driving instead of the pain. I think if Dylan wasn't sitting he might faint. I giggle at that thought and soon the pain ebbs. "Almost there," I say.

"Fuck, we almost died there for a minute, Andy," Dylan yells at me. "I can't believe you convinced me to let you drive." His hands still grip the dashboard and I have to steel myself from giggling. It was just a little push on the peddle. Geez. You'd think I gunned it.

"We did not. I totally had the situation handled. I just sped up a bit that's all. Stop being so dramatic." He opens his mouth to argue with me, but then thinks better of it. I pull up to the front of the hospital and get out. We'll worry about the car later. Right now, we need some assistance because the way these contractions are rolling through me, I think this baby is going to be popping out soon. "UGH!"

I lean against the car as Dylan gets out and hobbles to me and begins rubbing my back. "It's okay, baby. I've got you."

I breathe and breathe and breathe some more. It's not really helping. I wail out the pain. That seems to help. It puts Dylan in a tizzy though.

"Nurse!"

An older round nurse walks out with a wheelchair like this is a walk in the park. She spins the chair around like a pro and helps lower me into it.

"I think my husband might need one too. His ankle might be broken." The nurse looks at my husband and then down to his swollen ankle that now looks pretty hideous with its black and blue color. She whistles and a young nurse pops out of the automatic doors and then my husband and I are wheeled into the hospital.

They bring Dylan into x-ray while I move to the maternity floor. They promise he'll be here soon after I tell them this baby isn't coming out without her father. "You got it, sweetie," the nurse replies.

21

*D*ylan's x-rays don't take long at all. He just has a sprain, so they put his ankle in a boot and pull up a seat for him next to my bed. I'm wearing one of those hideous gowns that hospitals provide. I mean someone who died must've worn this at some point, right? I should've been like one of those moms that brings her own hospital gown. I just couldn't be bothered, but now I'm regretting my decision for fashionable hospital wear.

The contractions are stacking up and I'm feeling the urge to push. This girl feels like she's coming out whether we're ready or not. "Oh, we haven't decided on a name, Dylan!" We've been in a disagreement on what to call her since we knew she existed. We've also both changed our mind so many times, it's hard to keep up.

"It's okay, princess. Maybe, once we meet her we'll know."

I sigh in relief. That makes total sense. I mean what if we decided on Gertrude and she comes out and looks more like an Emily or something. I smile at him. My husband is so thoughtful. Another contraction comes and I bear down and squeeze his hand.

"Shit."

I let go of his hand and see it now resembles a lobster claw.

"Sorry."

He just shakes his head and kisses mine. "It's okay, baby. You're in a lot of pain. Give me some too." He laughs.

The doctor flitters in light as a fairy and snaps on her gloves and before I know it, she has my legs spread and is telling me to push. I wail and scream through every one of them. Dylan's face is priceless. He looks terrified. I wish I had my phone so I could take a picture. Then, I'm pushing again. Five more pushes and she's out.

"Welcome to the world, little one," my doctor says.

I smile at the little blob of goo, blood, and hair. She's so precious. Out of the corner of my eye, I see Dylan crying. I pretend not to see. The delivery nurse rubs her down, weighs her, checks her vitals and makes a little foot print on paper with ink. Then she's bundled in my arms with her eyes closed.

"She's so beautiful," Dylan says as he looks down into my arms. I nod and look at her small little face, trying to think of a name fit for this little girl.

"What should we name her?" I look up to Dylan. He shakes his head.

"I just keep thinking of the word beautiful," he replies.

I smile and look down at my girl. Her eyes are open a little. I tilt my head and think of the perfect name for her.

"How about Rose?"

Dylan gives me a huge grin.

"You're naming our baby girl Pink?" He laughs.

I nod my head completely serious. "I love it."

Dylan kisses me on the lips. "Well done, Mama."

"How are you doing, Daddy?"

Dylan kisses me again and grins. "I like that."

"I'm sure you do." I giggle. He leans his head against mine and we stare down at this little human we made together.

~

Rose Petal Ryder came into our lives and made it so much better. Birdie adores her. She like to sleep next to her on the couch. Any kind of coo that Rose makes, Birdie comes running, as does her father. The next day he went out and got a tattoo with her name and a beautiful pink rose on his chest. Yup, Dylan Ryder has a pink tattoo. Three points for Team Pink!

Dylan rocks our sweet Rose to sleep every night. I love watching them together, my husband and my child, our little family. We've been talking about getting a bigger place for our growing family. I'd love to decorate a place that belongs to both of us, and of course there will be pink.

Our parents never ended up marrying, thank God. Shortly after our confrontation, they broke up. I guess they saw the error in their ways. My dad calls me sometimes to check on baby Rose. He hasn't made a visit yet, but I told him he's always welcome.

Dylan's mother on the other hand, hasn't contacted us at all. That's how we like it. She's probably out on the ocean on a cruise. Maybe she's more of an Ursula? If only an iceberg would come around and bump her off the ship. I feel bad for her really. She didn't know how good she had it. Elizabeth probably still doesn't realize what she lost. Dylan's wonderful. I couldn't imagine having this baby without him. He's been so supportive and caring.

I think back to those days not long ago when we fought at our old accounting firm. We really were crazy about each other. The numbers might not have added up but we figured it out between the spreadsheets.

PLAYLIST

1. New Song- Warpaint
2. Delicate- Taylor Swift
3. Still falling for you- Ellie Goulding
4. Sit Next to Me- Foster the People
5. Ashes- Celine Dion
6. Tears that I Cry- Ariana Grande
7. Don't go Breaking my Heart- Backstreet Boys
8. Habits- Tove Lo
9. In My Blood- Shawn Mendes
10. Back To You- Selena Gomez
11. For You- Rita Ora & Liam Payne

EPILOGUE

Dylan

This pink tornado came barreling though my life and upended everything. She's a force of nature and I love her more than she knows. I looked forward to those days in the old office. I'd annoy her just to get a rise out of her. I knew exactly what I was doing. This girl made me crazy. She's too good for me. I just couldn't help myself. I needed something, anything from her, even if it was wrath. I laugh at how mad she used to get at me.

Looking at her now, she's pregnant with our second child and playing with our toddler in the kitchen. They're making cookies with pink and white chocolate chips. It's adorable. We don't know if we're having a boy or a girl yet, but I think it's a boy. She's carrying this one a bit different and her cravings are completely the opposite of what they were before. I love being here for all of it.

Our little Rose is just like her mama. She loves the color pink and will only wear dresses. I feel so sorry for Birdie. Rose puts her in the most ridiculous outfits. We even caught her putting lipstick on Birdie one day. That pig loves her to death though. They sleep together. Birdie used to be attached to me, following me like a lost dog. Not anymore, I've been totally forgotten, well not completely. She still likes a belly rub every once in a while.

Rose takes ballet classes. I can't help smile when I see her at practice in her little tutu. She has the same light brown hair as her mama. She has my eyes though. I'd like to think there's a little of me in there somewhere. I really don't mind having a smaller version of Andy. It's double the fun around here.

Andy made all this possible. I remember our relationship changing when she came to work for me. Yes, I thought she was a princess, but I found out how caring and weird she is. I love her weird. It's definitely my kind of weird. She plays video games better than I do for Christ's sake. I love little things like that about her.

It seemed like every day we worked together I'd found out another little treasure about her. I wasn't kidding when I said she moved around like she was dancing. It's really like a ballet watching her. That day it hit me and I had to get out of the office and get some fresh air. I hadn't ever felt that way about anyone, ever. It was like an emotional overload. I tried to keep my distance after that for a while, but Andy's charms never cease.

And after I had a taste of that sweetness, I was a goner.

The way I took her that first night, I was completely out of control. I had no choice but to make love to this woman. God, I wanted to feel her soft body against mine. I wanted her hands all over my body. I'd dreamed of that moment for years, since I first laid eyes on her that day I visited her in HR.

She was a petite little thing organizing all these boxes in her new office. She'd thrown up some girly pictures and a colorful pillow. It looked a lot better than it did before, that's for sure. No way in hell was I going to tell her that. I watched her for a moment.

Her light brown hair fell in her face. She pushed it back and I saw these luscious lips I just wanted to devour. Even the little sigh that fell from her lips gave me a hard-on. I just stood there like a dope ogling her. Her tight pencil skirt didn't help matters either and she wore a little pink polo that matched the shade of her lips. Don't even get me started on her black heels that I wanted wrapped around my waist.

She finally looked up at me with a questioning look in her eye. I figured she probably caught me staring. It put me on the defensive and I said some things I shouldn't have and then she returned with some venom of her own and that's how our beautiful relationship was born.

I look at her now, swollen with my child and shake my head at how I got so lucky. I'm just some kid who was good with numbers, who happened to work at the accounting firm she got hired at. I've tried to figure out this equation of how we even happened. I guess it's the one equation I can't figure out. She'll be forever my unsolved. I can't wait to spend the rest of my life trying figuring her out.

The End

ACKNOWLEDGMENTS

First, I just want to say a HUGE thank you to my friends and family for being so supportive. They only just recently found out that I write. Already, they've said how proud they are. It means the world to me.

Second, I want to thank the Indie community for helping a noob to fulfill her dreams. This really is a great community to be a part of. We stick together through thick and thin. Y'all are amazing! Thank you, Dani Antoinette for your help in the Chicago area. Please go check out her book, Wild Talk. It's HOT! Thank you, Bobby Kim for your continued guidance and being a genius leader for us author noobs.

Third, and most important, I want to thank Adam. You've been there for me from the beginning. Your faith never wavered. Your support means the world to me. I couldn't do this without you. I love you so much.

Also, to you wonderful reader, who've read this far and

took time out of your day to read my book. You gave me your time. I hope I gave you a steamy read in return. THANK YOU!

ABOUT THE AUTHOR

Nicky lives in the Big D, Dallas, Texas that is. She loves reading romantic books with sexy times and loves writing them even more. Nicky is a ninja, stationery addict, and a movie buff. She eats cookie dough while she writes. If you like long walks on the beach, steamy books with sexy man candy then Nicky is your girl.

Nicky's Socials:
Facebook
Twitter
Instagram

I have a reader group on Facebook where I love to do Giveaways and talk books.
Come hang out with us in the Vixen Den. I hope to see you there.
Nicky's Reader Group

If you're not on social media much but would love to know when I have a new release coming up or a giveaway, sign up for my newsletter. (No spam. I promise)

Nicky's Newsletter

ALSO BY NICKY FOX

My Pinup Girl

My Hookup Girl

Coming soon:

My Curvy Girl

The Priest's Mate

Printed in Great Britain
by Amazon